A Perfect Fantasy

MARK AESCHLIMANN

ISBN: 978-1-7636368-4-2

For those whose mind blocks their heart.

For those whose past prevents their future.

For me and my healing.

Chapter One

Will

'Pleeeaaase tell me you've found another girl to swoon over, Will. I'm getting soooo bored,' Davey moaned overly-dramatically.

'Only in the insanity that is my imagination, unfortunately. Oh, and those hot FMC's that everyone's got me reading now. Swoony swoony swoon,' Will replied with more than a hint of sarcasm as they awaited their much desired coffee, dodging the oncoming sidewalk traffic like pros. 'I just don't have time anymore. With the work and the other work and the marketing of the other work and the building of my braaaaand.' Will stuck out his tongue faux-vomit style as he ran his hands through his salt and pepper hair— no longer the dark brown it had been prior to a few years ago. The colouring of his closely trimmed beard matched the signs that forty was fast approaching.

'But you need some adventure… Excitement!' Jazz hands in full flow as Davey acted out his Broadway dreams with a few kicks and a suggestive glance. 'So do I, for that matter.'

'Well, at least we've still got each other, right?'

'No offence, Will, but you're not quite giving me what I need. You've rebuffed my advances for the last time!'

The coffee girl—Torah—stood at the window with coffees in hand, waiting for Will and Davey to finish their pantomime. She had long since moved beyond being confused by their oddly dramatic conversations.

'At least you both give me a reason to come to work every morning,' she said with a smile. 'Never dull while you're around. So cute with your little matching jeans and black shirts.'

'Why, thank you m'lady,' Davey curtsied as he took his coffee, popping the brownie treat into his mouth. 'I could've been a star, you know.' He batted his eyelashes playfully in her direction.

'There's still time,' she replied, giggling. 'You guys have a great day. See you tomorrow.'

Will took his travel cup from Torah with a smile. 'As always, our queen of elixirs,' he bowed his head slightly as he turned away to begin their short walk back to the office.

Davey read the hand-written message on the lid of his coffee. '"May today be as bright as your smile." Awwwwwwww. See Will, this is why I need to keep getting these disposable cups. I can't get this dopamine hit anywhere else.'

'Mmm-hmm,' Will replied while chewing on his brownie.

Reaching the entrance of Dreams To Reality—the small advertising agency where they worked—both Will and Davey stopped, dramatically sighed, and walked through the door.

'Chat later,' Davey said as they reached Will's desk.

'Later,' Will replied knowing full well that a message was only minutes away via the office chat.

In one swift motion Will placed his coffee on the desk, put his headphones over his black-rimmed glasses and sat down. Silencing the noise was a requirement for him to be able to concentrate and do his job with a focussed mind and minimal interruption.

By day Will was primarily a website developer, and occasional app developer, whilst also being the go-to guy for all manner of technical questions relating to office technology—the clear pathway following the completion of his university degree.

As the code flowed through his fingers, to his screen, he took regular glances out the window to check on the weather. Some unseasonal rains had hit late spring and was putting his lunchtime walk in jeopardy. His walks acted as both a reset for his mind, to get through the afternoon, and an attempt to keep his skin slightly tanned. With Christmas approaching, and with it the Australian heat and UV, retaining enough colour in his skin made him at least feel like he was spending enough time outside.

Will never thought himself attractive—physically or his personality. In fact he had always found himself to be particularly average beyond his height alone. He had succumbed to depression and let himself go physically for a long time.

As he approached the big 4-0, however, Will was determined to finish his thirties in a manner that could propel him forward positively in his forties. He had made many changes and come a long way toward getting into shape. Still on the journey but far enough along that he took great pride in his progress. That made an enormous difference to his health and self esteem and Will was finally finding himself in a better place mentally—slight work burnout aside.

Will and Davey went for a quick mental-health debrief beverage at the end of the day. A small team made the work intense at times and given the personality of both Will and Davey, they took it personally when any issues arose.

'Okay, what are we having?' Davey asked.

'The usual. Red. Need now,' Will replied, exhausted, placing his bag down on one of the four chairs surrounding a small table, before taking a seat himself.

On this occasion they went to the closest bar to work—The Corner Office—a small classic-looking bar renovated with dark wood and a large alfresco area. The selection wasn't their favourite but met the needs of the moment.

Davey headed straight for the bar to order, putting on his usual account manager charm to schmooze the bar staff. Much like Will, Davey was on a journey of getting his life back in order, putting in the work after a tumultuous period to get his mind and body back to the glory days of his youth. His ginger hair ensured he stood out in a crowd despite his short stature.

In stark contrast to Will, however, Davey's peak excellence came in being a people-person. A hit on any dance floor—as opposed to Will's awkwardness—and a danger to any timid man who dared enter his domain, Davey was well known at a number of clubs around town from his younger days.

Both men had become an important part of each other's recovery—Davey pushing Will in the social arena where he struggled the most, and Will giving Davey a like-mind to discuss interests outside of work, as well as giving him regular self-esteem boosts by reminding him of how awesome and helpful he was.

Davey quickly returned to the table with a glass of Syrah in each hand, placing them down before taking a breath.

'Okay…can you believe what Shenae did? She railroaded the entire project and set us back weeks. I had everything sorted and signed off and she just steps in and rips it apart. What the hell?'

'I know. Screw the deadline, hey? I assume it isn't shifting?' Will asked, already knowing the answer.

'Of course not. I could-' Davey took a deep breath. 'Calm down Davey… Deep breaths. We'll work it out.'

'You always do, Davey. The place would fall apart without you.'

'Nawww. Thanks Will. You're the one that delivers though.'

Both cheers'd their glasses and took a soothing sip of wine.

'So what do you have planned for the weekend?' Will asked.

'Not a whole lot. Got an invite to a party but not sure if I wanna go. I don't really know the people that well.'

'And that stopped you, when?' Will asked with a giggle.

'This is true. Not sure I need the long night though. Need me some relaxation time. What are you doing? Do I need to ask?'

'Probably not,' Will joined Davey in a laugh knowing how predictable he was.

'More reading. More writing. Groceries, gym, watch my football team.'

'So the exact same as every weekend?'

'Pretty much,' Will replied.

'As long as it's making you happy. You just need to promise that when you're famous you take me with you.'

'I promise that in that very unlikely event, you can ride my coat-tails.'

'Perfect. And when you're paying me to take care of all your marketing needs you can get back on the prowl,' Davey purred as he made a clawing gesture, causing Will to laugh.

'Not sure about that, Davey. That requires actually talking to people.'

'But you're great with words, Will.'

'Which puts me in the perfect position for when we return to carrier pigeons. Until that time I can write a hell of a message and fail in person.'

Despite progress made, Will's anxiety went into overdrive when he had to hold a conversation with a stranger. It took a long time for him to warm up enough to be open in a conversation and he still regularly found himself stammering over his words. Another reason Will loved having Davey around was for him to be that social buffer. A well placed and executed joke helped Will relax without having to do the bulk of the talking, expediting the process of him opening up.

Not that any of that could help with matters of the heart. Messaging on an app was the easy part. Meeting in person was where things fell apart—he struggled to get past the anxiety of instant feedback and the lack of ability to proof and edit before pressing send. It wasn't that anyone thought he was rude—as many people had years earlier when he could barely speak at all— Will just didn't have the time he needed for people to get to know him properly, so things ended before they could begin.

'Most people already see you for the kind and wholesome person you are. They just think you're not interested in them because you don't talk to them,' Davey said, trying to pick up Will's spirits.

'Yeah? Where's the receipts? I need written references,' Will laughed awkwardly.

After a few silent moments of Davey not acknowledging the self-deprecating humour, Will gave Davey the honesty he was looking for. 'I know, Davey. I am who I am and I'm not ashamed of that. Those things people perceive as weaknesses make me really good at other things. Whether people want to see that or not is up to them. I'm not going to market myself as something else just to trick someone into being with me. It's dishonest and it's probably not the type of person I want to be with anyway.' Will shrugged as he trailed off and sipped his wine.

'Nobody's going to have a problem if you embellish a little just to grease the wheels,' Davey added.

'I will. It's not me. If I find someone she'll know who I am. No deceit—no embellishments.'

'And if you don't get any bites?'

'Then they'll miss out on me and I can sleep guilt-free—albeit alone.'

Will was steadfast in how he would find the one for him.

'I respect that, you big teddy bear,' Davey said wiping faux-tears with a napkin before throwing it at Will.

'What about you? When are you gonna settle down?' Will asked knowing the answer—regardless of its honesty. It wasn't the first time they'd had this exchange.

'When I find a man that can handle me—yet none have proven to be up to the task,' Davey glanced up and down at a new patron in the establishment who had just walked through the door—a cheeky smile appearing at the tight jeans and even tighter white t-shirt he was wearing.

Will knew Davey wanted the same as him. Someone to love him for who he was. Where they differed was how they would spend their time until that day came. It wasn't lost on Will that the man had glanced back—the corners of his mouth rising in acknowledgment.

'Looks like you could do with a free seat so I will take my leave and catch you next week.' Will stood and picked up his bag.

'You don't have to go, Will.' Davey sounded almost apologetic although Will knew it was just pretence and cocked his head to one side—calling out the bullshit.

'Thank you,' Davey whispered as Will patted him on the shoulder, before taking his leave.

Every evening Will returned home to his apartment, which he had kept since his divorce. Living a relatively solitary existence was most comfortable for him—even during his marriage—and allowed him the peace to fulfil his passion—writing. Will had a knack for thinking up stories based on the most mundane of situations. He had no doubt this was a result of his introverted personality and lifelong battle with anxiety. Risk mitigation came with thinking up every possible scenario no matter how insane it seemed. Wandering down a rabbit-hole in his mind was a normal occurrence for him.

After a session in the gym, followed by dinner, Will sat down at his desk and allowed himself to get caught up in the latest world he was creating. Never one to shy away from his love of geek culture, he gravitated toward fantasy and science fiction regardless of the form of media.

The release from the constraints he was required to put on his imagination during the day allowed him to fully relax. Being home, getting lost in his writing, allowed Will to feel free. He knew it was a defence mechanism to avoid the disappointments and anxieties of the rest of the world—therapy had taught him as much—but putting distance between himself and his long-time nemesis, DnA as he called it, was intoxicating in itself.

Depression and anxiety were always lurking, a daily struggle to combat, like the evil powers within his stories. Picking his own battles had become his strategy as opposed to letting others dictate how he should live. He'd learned that there was no shame in playing to his strengths and it made for a far more open, transparent, and approachable Will than he had been in the past. That and finding great mental health buddies, like Davey.

Will smiled as he tapped away at his keyboard, the valve released on his creative juices and living in his element.

Chapter Two

Jess

'Any new book boyfriends?' Cait asked while pouring herself a large black coffee from the pot only she used. Despite the years of living in Australia she was still yet to let go of the filtered coffee she frequently dieted on in her native US.

'Since yesterday?' Jess answered—a small smirk emerging. 'Of course. Always need a few on the go at a time.'

Jess was also making herself a coffee, although by way of showing off her barista skills on the coffee machine that the staff at the library managed to negotiate, courtesy of most of the Christmas party budget—a small sacrifice with no regrets from anyone. Both sat down at the staffroom table briefly for a welcome short break.

'Maybe you could do with one or two of the real variety on the go at a time? Just for a regularly scheduled service, of course. Get the engine working, rotate the tires, drain and change the fluids. Maintenance is important,' Cait broke out into laughter at the grossed out reaction on Jess' face. Having been brought up on a rural farm, machine maintenance analogies were run-of-the-mill from Cait.

'Eww,' was all Jess could manage to muster before also bursting into laughter—her loose, blonde curls bouncing. It was extremely clear when Jess found anything humorous. Her entire body always joined in—along with the occasional snort.

'I think I'm good, Cait. When I find a worthy prince I'll let you know.' Jess was steadfast in her independence until she found someone who could remotely live up to the expectations she found in her books. She didn't think it was too much to ask to find a hot guy who would tear down the universe for her, while simultaneously shedding his bad-boy persona, and be content with waiting an eternity for the briefest of touches.

Jess definitely had her share of suitors over the years. She was pretty by all accounts—and had more than enough references from people who thought so. One thing she was never prepared to do, though, was settle for one of the misogynistic arseholes that she had succumbed to converse with on the rare occasion on a dating app, in a bar, or—rarer still—an actual date. Nobody had yet managed to clear the first, low hurdle, and with every failure her barriers strengthened.

Growing up, fantasy stories were an integral part of Jess' life and she was now very much in her romantasy era in her mid-thirties. Her love of magic and fae—and the accompanying genre—was ever-present in her choice of attire from the youngest age and wasn't going anywhere—whether that be for cosplay or every-day dress. At the very least she needed to have some kind of branding or imagery on an item of clothing. It was her and she loved it that way.

As did the children she regularly hosted for group activities in the library. While half of her job was re-shelving and checking books in and out, the other half was preparing for, and hosting, book-based activities for schools or private groups. They were specifically fantasy related as that was her expertise. So much so that finding books to stock in the library was not officially part of her job, however her opinion was regularly sought when it came to stocking that genre.

On this particular day Jess' blonde hair and light skin was striking in contrast to the emerald-green linen dress with a square neck and short butterfly sleeves. The dress was tied off above her waist with a cream sash. Her hair was held from her brown eyes by a plastic green headband moulded on top with a leafy pattern.

Cait, on the other hand, always dressed casual with jeans, a t-shirt and sneakers. She quickly washed her mug before walking behind Jess and gently wrapping her arms around her shoulders.

'It's Friday, Jess. Please come out with us after work. You'll have a great time.'

'I know I'll have a great time…for a while. Then some guy—or guys—will ruin it or someone will get drunk and start to tell me how to live my life.'

'I did that one time,' Cait defended herself.

'Yes. You did that one time. If it's not you it's someone else. I don't understand why people think I can't be happy because I live my life differently to them. Sure, someone might be nice occasionally but I don't need anyone. I also don't need to get trashed and get laid. I'm happy at home with a book…or books… lots and lots of books,' Jess smiled briefly. 'I get it enough when I'm with the family. I don't need it when I'm out with mates as well.'

'I know, Jess. And I love that about you. I still need to check in from time to time though.'

Jess placed a hand on Cait's hand, which was still resting on her shoulder. 'Thanks, Cait. Feel free to run interference with the guys though.' Both women laughed as they stood to return to work.

Most misjudged Jess as a woman who lacked confidence, and someone who lived a safe life due to her preference for quiet reading over a night out. In reality Jess was just tired of trying to justify her life choices to those who simply couldn't understand—and usually didn't even bother to try.

Her friends understood her position. Most of them shared her love of books—although not quite to the same extent—which gave them more perspective than her family. It's why she was happy enough to join them for coffee, meals and even the occasional night of drinks when she'd much prefer to be reading.

While she was present with them she was full of stories, jokes and laughter. They were also—mostly—understanding when she left before everyone else. It was expected and they knew nothing would make her change.

"Bubbly" and "warm" were often used to describe her personality regardless of the company she was with. Friends, family, colleagues and library regulars all saw Jess in the same manner.

Jess' insistence on treating everybody equally allowed them to experience her as her authentic self—even if it was slightly dialled up around her friends. She couldn't exactly talk as openly—or descriptively—about her spicy books with her grandparents, although in recent times conversation at family gatherings had turned entirely to the upcoming wedding of her brother, James, and Audrey.

Despite a relatively recent engagement, the wedding was only a few short months away—enough time to work off the Christmas indulgences before digging into yet another feast.

She was always close with her big brother—James being two years older—and got along well with Audrey, whose personality was similar to James.

While Audrey didn't have the same commitment to books as Jess—her job, as well as James, and the upcoming wedding taking up all her time—she was always interested when chatting to Jess about all the fantastic worlds she was discovering—including the spicy ones.

All things considered Jess was extremely happy with where her life was and very much looking forward to the wedding—allowing her to dream up all manner of whimsical scenarios that would likely never come to pass.

Throughout the afternoon, after the request was initially made during their lunch break, Cait slowly wore Jess down until she finally relented and agreed to join her for drinks that evening. With summer having arrived the sun was yet to disappear as Jess, Cait and a few other colleagues took one of the last remaining tables in their go-to outdoor bar—The Green Vine.

Jess had added a light yellow denim jacket to her ensemble knowing a nighttime chill in the air was still ever-present until the full heat of summer crept in. Unintentionally she had become the picture of summer at the venue amongst so many who were professionally dressed.

Being a sunny evening the group started on the white wines along with some share plates of cheese, crackers and croquettes. The fairy lights amongst the ornamental vines were beginning to take effect as the surrounding building cast shadows inside the inner-city bar. Being early still the music volume was yet to be lifted giving the ambience that Jess loved. Everybody was in a joyous mood as they could chat, joke and laugh without a shout to disrupt the mood.

As the evening slowly rolled on, space seemed to get tighter around Jess and the volume incrementally increased—both from the music and the patrons—and Jess left her friends on the dance floor to take a break at a small table recently vacated. Twilight turned to night and, for a brief moment, Jess was able to block her ears and look up to a beautifully lit canopy of foliage hoping that everyone would be transported away to be replaced by a fae knight —come to take her heart and become her world.

Her sojourn to the faraway land came crashing to an end with the rattling of empty glasses and rocking of the table. A sigh and an eye-roll met the well trimmed and sculpted man who had taken it upon himself to commandeer the seat next to Jess. The business attire with rolled up sleeves, square jaw and recently curated hair —along with the over-exposure of cologne—told Jess all she needed to know about the type of guy who would have the confidence—nay arrogance—to sit next to her without even the pretence of asking permission.

'Hey. How you goin'? What're you doin' sitting here on your own?' he asked, resting his head upon his fist, elbow on the table.

Not wanting to seem antagonistic Jess answered hoping he'd get the hint that what he was looking for wasn't on the cards.

'Hi. Just having a few drinks with my friends. Ladies only night. You understand, right?'

'Yeah. I'm here with a few of the boys from the office. Have a few bevvies and see where the night takes us. Gotta live it up on a Friday night, am I right?'

'If that's your thing, then I guess you're right. I'm just here to spend some time with friends.'

'Right. But you're not with your friends. I'm sure I could be great company for ya. I'm Shano, by the way,' he said, beginning to edge closer.

Jess smiled awkwardly and looked at anything but him.

'I'm in finance. Had a successful year. Thinking about taking a trip to celebrate. Maybe a resort, a bit of sun. Make a great summer out of it. Would be great with a bit of company and someone special to take care of. What's your name? What do you do for work?'

If he was going to persist, then Jess would at least make him squirm—having summed up the odds that he'd respond the way she thought. 'I'm Tasneem.' Jess noticed him recoil immediately despite Shano trying to hide it.

While she took no pleasure in using another culture in this way it was an easy way to firstly, see if he would surprise her; and secondly, make him exit post-haste if he lived up to expectations.

'I work in admin in a local migrant center,' Jess continued. 'My family came here when I was just a-'

'Sorry, my mate's just called me from the bar. Chat later?' Shano stood up even quicker than he sat down and walked as quickly as he could to the indoor portion of the venue.

'But you didn't get to hear about my fifty siblings and welfare! Great talk, bigot!' Jess called out after him.

Cait sat down next to Jess, judgement painted all over her face. 'Having fun?'

'What? I didn't do anything,' Jess put on her most innocent face while trying as best she could suppress a cheeky grin.

Cait's eyebrows raised. 'He looked cute.'

'And?' Jess replied—her own eyebrows raised.

'Nobody cares about the personality of their plumber.'

Jess burst into laughter and a snort prompted Cait to also lose control.

'He was the usual arsehole, Cait. I didn't even get to finish my story before he ran away,' Jess shrugged innocently, yet both knew it was no surprise.

'And run away he did…extremely quickly…Tasneem. What would you have done if he reacted differently?' Cait asked.

'Firstly, Cait, he make it pretty clear what he was looking for; and secondly, if—by some miracle—I got him completely wrong I would tell him the truth, and he would understand completely because he would have empathy. As it stands he's a rich douchebag with no empathy who just wanted a bangin' summer… which he can have with someone else. Does it give me an icky feeling to have done it? Yes, but he wouldn't take the hint.'

'I'll admit, Jess, that you have a one hundred percent record at working these guys out since I've met you.'

'Fool me once,' Jess said, her tone becoming serious.

'And yet nobody can shed their bad-boy persona if you don't let a bad-boy in.'

'Well, when the bad-boy comes with wings, pointy ears or a natural skin colour we've never seen before we can reassess. While we live in the real world these bad-boys have no redeeming qualities as far as I can see. Definitely not at our age. That shit's baked in at this point.'

'I think a masquerade ball will get you. The next day you'll turn up with the biggest of glows,' Cait said with a chuckle.

'Is your favourite pastime finding ways of getting me laid?' Jess asked, joining in the laugh.

'It's pretty high up there. I love a challenge.'

'Well, unfortunately for you that challenge will continue as I call it a night.'

'Really? But the night's so young,' Cait put on her pouty face knowing full-well that there was nothing that would change Jess' mind.

'My men await…' Jess laughed as she stood to take her leave and spend the rest of the night with her books.

Chapter Three

Jess

The weekend had been a quiet one for Jess. For the most part she spent her time in the sanctuary of her inner-city townhouse, which she rented from James since he had moved in with Audrey. Chores were slowly knocked off throughout Saturday.

Sunday morning brought with it family breakfast at her parents' house in the suburbs. In recent times it had also doubled-up as wedding planning with Audrey. Jess took an interest in the preparations and was happy to provide her fantastical suggestions whenever asked upon.

James and Audrey had decided that perfectly simple was the way to go for them. While expensive—not an issue for them as their jobs more than covered that area—the decision making was heavily reduced in order to reduce stress and enjoy the experience.

The added benefit was that they could grow closer while Jess' mum and grandmother still had enough to fuss over instead of casting judgement on the love-life—or lack thereof—of Jess. Audrey played the blocker perfectly by finding small details for them to work through, which Jess greatly appreciated. Comments that she needed to find someone had taken a welcome downturn.

This allowed Jess to go into the new week in an even more spirited mood than usual.

'You're looking buoyant,' Cait observed with a smile.

'What can I say? My weekend wasn't ruined by discussion regarding who I was or wasn't dating for the first time in forever.'

Jess was giddy with joy at having experienced the dream of a relaxing weekend, lived on her terms.

'Whaaaaaat? I don't believe you. How could this be?' Cait's sarcasm was no match for Jess' mood to begin the week.

'Luckily for me the wedding planning is in full swing so everyone was too distracted or busy to bring it up. We could actually just sit at a table as a family without the topic coming up. I can't even begin to tell you how rejuvenating that was.'

'You don't need to tell me, Jess. I can see it pretty clearly and I, for one, am here for it.' Cait raised a hand in the air to be slapped enthusiastically by a jumping Jess as they giggled.

Jess' bubbly disposition permeated throughout the rest of the library as both staff and visitor alike revelled in the positive vibes. There were no activities planned for the morning which gave the staff the opportunity to relax into the week. The tasks that were usually more on the mundane side were done with a skip in their step.

Jess' mood also brought with it a change in her usual attire, which ordinarily leaned hard on her love of fantasy. Instead of sporting a fantasy-inspired dress she had opted for a simple ensemble of jeans, sneakers and t-shirt—although the white t-shirt was adorned with a large book, fairies and their sparkling magic.

The lunch break arrived quicker than usual given the mood in the building.

'So, Cait, what did you get up to on the weekend?' Jess asked. Cait's quick matching of the vibe suggested to Jess that she, too, had a good weekend.

'Well, as you know it was my housemate's birthday and we went out for dinner at that fancy new French place up the street from us. The guy at the bar was sooooo cute. Spanish, light stubble, slight tan, firm arm as observed by the old laugh and touch play. Naturally I was happy to make very frequent drink orders for the table.'

'On a librarian salary?' Jess asked, shocked at how she could afford such extravagance.

'Of course not. Her parents had a tab going,' Cait corrected, causing both to laugh. 'Anyway, I was my usual sparkling self and dressed ever so stunningly to hit the club later. I could see there was a little something there—glances from the other side of the restaurant. So I blew him a kiss as we left and let it simmer, planning to grace the establishment with my patronage at a later date. Well, unbeknownst to myself, Sarah had dropped word to him on the way out as to where we were heading.'

'What a fortunate turn of events,' Jess pointed out as she brewed herself a fresh coffee.

'Fortunate indeed, although one could say the fortune was all in his favour,' Cait responded with a smirk.

'Oh, Cait, whatever do you mean?' Jess asked slyly, eyeing, with annoyance, the intruder who had entered the room.

Their colleague—Steve from IT—had no idea what he had walked in on when initially placing his mug in the queue to brew his own coffee. He slowly backed up to the door for a hasty exit, understanding the coded holding pattern of the conversation via the vernacular of a bygone era.

The door handle rotating back to its original position was the cue for the conversation to return. Jess stared in expectation.

'My dear Jessica, coitus was had of course,' Cait's overly dramatic smug laugh was completed with a sip of coffee with pointed pinky.

'Ok. Enough of that,' Jess said leaning in. 'Details pleeeease.'

'A lady does not bang then sang,' Cait continued the pretence.

'One, nobody has ever accused you of being *a lady*,' Jess corrected with all the toitiness she could muster. 'Two, *bang then sang* is your modus operandi and always has been.'

'This is fair. Okay. So we get to the club and we're all having a great time, drinks and dancing, you know how we are. Suddenly I feel a tap on my shoulder as we're dancing away. I turn and there he is. His smile… Ahhhhhhhhh his smile. A very quick drink later we're back on the dance floor and I'm getting the first of many examples of how he can move his hips.'

'Aaaaand you got his number this time, right? Not like the last few,' Jess enquired, although the tone of the conversation suggested she hadn't forgotten this time.

'Yes I did, like the lady that I am.' The pinky, once again, making an appearance.

'So what else is he like?' Jess asked. 'Aside from the tantalisingly mobile hips.'

'Well, as it happens, he also loves cooking. His job right now is a stepping stone to becoming a chef. Imagine if we'd met on my cheffing travels. I may never had ended up here.' Cait tapped her chin in contemplation of what could have been in a previous life.

'Maybe,' Jess responded sceptically. 'But you gave that life up for a reason, so it's probably better this way. Are you worried about finding the time to see each other if he did become a chef? That's assuming you continue to see each other, of course.'

'After a single, spicy night of passion? Not so much.' Both laughed as the two ladies finished their coffee and left the break room.

Upon turning the corner in the hallway, Cait gave a shout. 'Steve! We're done!'

Steve appeared from a storeroom—which lacked air-conditioning—sweaty yet relieved that he could finally get his coffee as he awkwardly scurried past them.

The afternoon brought with it the first of two children's group activities of the day. This one was a simple fancy dress for the children, who would dress as their favourite book character and give them an opportunity to talk to the group about the character and the book.

The activity was one of the simpler to organise for Jess as she only needed to provide some parameters and let the children and parents do all the work. The hardest task was making sure the others remained quiet and attentive while they each stood in front of the group and spoke in turn. Sometimes she had the added complexity of shy children, however in this group they were few and far between.

Being so close to Christmas a theme naturally emerged, although Jess knew this was mostly pushed onto the children by the parents who weren't looking to add to their long list of jobs by making a brand new outfit. As long as the children were enjoying themselves—and she could throw in some simple lessons on morals along the way—Jess didn't mind and was empathetic to the difficulties of the season.

The level of engagement from the parents Jess encountered in the library varied greatly. Some liked to use the group activities as an opportunity to get some child-free relaxation—café visits were often on the cards for small groups of them. Some tried to get as many errands done in the short time they had, leaving them flustered when they arrived to pick up their child—occasionally late. A few parents were very engaged in the activities organised by Jess. It wasn't uncommon for extra help in preparation and packing away to be given and as such Jess got to know some of the parents very well—especially those who had multiple children come through over the years.

The second activity was reading time where Jess read a book to the children—who were prone to falling asleep. This often made it an extremely quiet affair and an easy way to end the day. Jess made sure to always have a coffee before reading to the children to avoid falling asleep herself—a mistake which only needed to occur once before learning her lesson.

After the reading had been completed and the parents picked up their children, one of the mothers, Marie—who often helped Jess prepare and pack up—approached Jess with a strange smirk on her face.

'Hi, Jess. I hope everything went well today. You're dressed very differently than usual. I like it.'

'Thanks, Marie. Just changing it up a little. Feeling rejuvenated after the weekend,' Jess responded with a smile—albeit still a little confused by the look on Marie's face which was yet to change.

'So, I know you're usually not into this kind of thing, and feel free to say no, but I have a friend who recently came onto the market.' Marie seemed overly excited to share this particular piece of news with Jess, who was, most definitely, not one for blind dates —or being set up with friends of friends for that matter. Consequently, anxiety started brewing in the pit of her stomach.

'Oh. Thanks, Marie, bu-'

'I'm sure you'll like him. He owns a café and loves his coffee. He's a great cook, he reads and he's really quite handsome. I know it's not your thing but maybe consider meeting him?'

For a fleeting second Jess considered the proposal as the end of a good—albeit short—run of positive events. Instead she decided to go against her usual judgement and consider it a continuation of the positive trend, leaning into it. *Maybe I should ride this good luck I'm having,* she thought as excitement began to take over—an odd and out of character experience for her.

'You know what, Marie. I'll give it a go. I'm free on Friday night if he is.'

'You will? Yes! I'm so excited. I'll have a chat with Darren and let you know tomorrow,' Marie turned and walked out of the library with her son and the biggest smile Jess had ever seen grace her face.

'Darren?' Cait said walking over to Jess—eyebrows raised.

'I guess we'll see what happens,' Jess shrugged but couldn't help a smile escaping.

A slight smugness hit Cait's face. 'This is most unlike you, Jess. I'm liking it. Time to-'

'Please not a car analogy, Cait, we're going so well,' Jess laughed, with Cait joining in, as they packed away the last of the mats and chairs.

Chapter Four

Will

Another week came and went and Christmas party season was in full swing. A mid-week dinner at his parents' house ended in frustration at his dad's insistence that Will needed to find a girlfriend.

'Not really all on me,' Will responded. The fact that it took two people to make a couple seemingly lost on his dad. 'And anyway, I'm busy with my writing and trying to sell my book.'

'You can't just sit at home all the time and bury your head in the sand. You need to get out there.' Apparently the ongoing battle over Will's status was going to continue.

'Why exactly do I need to get out there, Dad?' Will didn't want to get into the difference between *want* and *need* as he'd done in the past. Preferring to be more subtle about his point this time around.

'I just told you, son. You can't sit at home all the time.'

'So is the issue that I can't sit at home all the time—assuming I actually sit at home all the time—or that I *need* a girlfriend?' Will asked rather sarcastically.

'Can't it be both? I just want you to be happy. We both do.' Will's dad nodded in his mum's direction as he spoke.

'I know you both do, Dad. But you keep telling me what I need to be happy. You don't ever ask me what makes me happy. We're not the same person and this isn't the same world you grew up in. I don't *need* anyone. Do I want someone? Sure. I also want to write my stories and have people enjoy them. I'm not willing to throw that away—as well as my mental health—by obsessing over finding someone. If it happens, it happens. If it doesn't, but I still get to do what makes me happy while spending my time with good people, then I'll still be happy. I get that you don't understand that but can you at least respect it?'

Will stood up from the dining table as his dad shook his head.

'Will, love, don't go home angry,' Will's mum interjected, trying to play peacemaker.

'I'm not angry, Mum. I'm just frustrated. I'm tired of people telling me what I need to be happy instead of letting me live my life. I don't come here for this.'

'I'm sorry, Will. Let me pack you some food to take home with you.'

'Thanks, Mum. I know you guys mean well but it's not helping when this gets brought up.'

Will gave his parents a hug and began the drive home. It was the kind of frustration that Will knew would eat at him for days. He knew they weren't entirely wrong. He knew why he struggled and bemoaned the fact that he couldn't have time to write, share his stories and find someone to love—who would love him just as much—without his mental health nose-diving in the process. To an extent he was burying his head in the sand—it just happened to be by doing something he loved to do.

Friday rolled around and Will and Davey were joined by a few other colleagues—Aisha, Alex and Mike—meaning a changeup in venue. The Green Vine was the consensus and they decided to get there early before the small area, which wasn't reserved for functions at that time of year, hit capacity.

Will loved hanging out with Davey, as he did often, but having a crew occasionally was a welcome change. He enjoyed the diversity of the group—which mirrored a large portion of the staff at Dreams To Reality—and threw up vastly different topics of conversation. Their different lives, different worlds and different jobs provided a much needed circuit-breaker to the occasional spiralling that could happen when it was just Will and Davey. Despite usually arriving in the same place, the origin was always different and Will had a lot of interest in how they all arrived at the destination—a dynamic which also helped give him perspective for his writing. The fact that they all shared the same baseline of how to treat people was what tied them all together.

A few days had passed to somewhat simmer the frustration from his mid-week altercation with his dad. The fact that everything was still kicking around his head, however, brought up anxiety he didn't need before heading out. Will was well-aware that his current headspace—along with a bar packed with seasonal jolliness, beautiful women and a few drinks—was a recipe for depression and loneliness. Importantly, Will had done the work to be aware of it and know when to walk away and distance himself. He also had Davey, and Davey had Will. They both looked out for each other and respected what the other needed and when.

The decision to go early turned out to be a smart one as they were able to take one of the few remaining tables available. The non-function area had quickly filled with people from local offices scurrying over as quickly as they could after they had finished work. All had the same idea as the crew from Dreams To Reality.

While Davey went to the bar for the first round Will was already organising the second round via the QR code on the table. None of the group were rookies to nights out in the busy season and knew that ordering well before required would give them a perfectly timed refill. In fact they had spent far too much of the day discussing the logistics behind the perfect ordering time at different periods of the year and varying venue types.

As tabs ran out at Christmas functions, the patrons drifted into the—already packed—general area, making The Green Vine grow exponentially louder as the evening wore on. It was quickly becoming impossible for Will to hear anyone speak above the noise of music and shouted discussions from the increased number of people jammed in. All sound had become a mass of unstructured noise invading Will's head.

It had become so packed that drunken patrons were regularly stumbling into Will's back and knocking their table. The claustrophobia was beginning to hit Will hard as his heart beat faster in his chest. Feeling the panic he attempted to breathe slowly. He closed his eyes and tried to block everything out, however the incessant noise blasting into his ears and echoing through his entire body rendered his attempts futile.

Will felt a hand on his and opened his eyes.

'Are you okay?' The words mouthed by Davey.

'Not really,' was Will's reply.

'You wanna get out of here?'

'Yeah.' Will knew his limit had long been exceeded and cursed himself for not taking his leave sooner, although he appreciated Davey for being on top of the situation. 'You guys stay if you're having a good time,' Will added. He hated ruining someone else's fun despite knowing a point was reached where it was out of his control.

'You guys hold the table. I'll be back,' Davey shouted as he and Will stood to leave.

Suddenly Will had something to focus on as he saw a self-proclaimed *alpha male* walk up to a—still seated—Alex and shout 'Take a look at this freak!'.

Will was naturally protective of anyone in his pack when they went out at night, becoming hyper-vigilant of his surroundings and his friends' safety the longer the night wore on. The resulting tradeoff in the enjoyment he experienced while being out with his friends often left him frustrated, despite his acceptance that this was just who he was regardless of whether he wanted to occasionally switch it off.

This character trait was one of the few things which would override his usual avoidance of confrontation—as well as his current state of near panic attack—as he quickly moved himself between Alex, seated at the end of the table, and the bigot standing over her—clearly unable to get past his own insecurities.

The man, taking offence to Will standing up to him, tried to push Will as one of his friends wrapped an arm around his waist to pull him back.

'He's just drunk,' his friend said, attempting to calm tensions.

'You think that's an excuse?' Will shouted back.

This resulted in the less intoxicated of the two men abandoning his lacklustre effort to pull his friend back, his thin veneer of rationality easily escaping him.

'Can't take a little heat, woke boy?' the initial aggressor shouted back.

'The only heat was in your pants, the way you clearly wanted her attention. But while we're having this chat, care to define what woke means?' Will's calm demeanour masked his inner turmoil.

'You're just a bunch of fucking snowflakes,' he shouted.

'What was that? Snowflakes? That was your definition? Quite the wordsmith we've got here. A cornucopia of knowledgeable takes,' Will was fully aware that his words were being drowned out, but also knew the computational power within their brains couldn't decipher how they were being mocked.

As was usual with these types of people the chests began to puff. They knew they had been humiliated, had no idea how, and that further emboldened their anger as they stepped closer to Will with an attempted flex of muscles.

Unbeknownst to the so-called *alphas* Alex was far taller than Will, a keen basketball player back in the day, and still enjoyed keeping fit. As she stood in the poorly-lit bar she towered over them and despite the lack of threat she posed, both in her persona and demeanour, the shocked pause allowed enough time for security to arrive and escort the drunk men out of the venue.

'Thanks, Will,' Alex said, giving him a hug. 'Although, I really didn't need the help.'

'I was already up,' Will laughed. 'Anyway, I'm heading off. This place is a bit too busy for me.'

Will said his goodbyes to the group as Aisha and Mike burst out laughing at the absurdity of the events that had just unfolded.

Will and Davey weaved through the crowd toward the exit. As space began to open Will could feel himself begin to calm. It was also at that point that Davey noticed Will's shoe was untied.

'Tie your shoe before you leave, Will. Don't want you tripping and falling into the lap of a beautiful woman, do we?'

Will laughed as he turned and lifted his foot onto the wall of a small raised garden bed to tie his shoe. As he did so Davey's attention was drawn away to a man walking into the venue wearing jeans, a black shirt and a leather jacket. He seemed to be South Asian in heritage with a fresh haircut and thin beard. Accompanying him was a blonde woman in jeans, flats and a white t-shirt which said *I left my boyfriend in my other books*. Davey chuckled at the t-shirt and turned to get Will's attention. By the time Will had finished tying his shoe and turned around they had disappeared into the crowd.

'Wish you could've seen the girl that just walked past lol. Definitely your bookish type, although accompanied by another man—a hot one I might add.'

'Great. Just my luck that not only would I miss the perfect woman walking by, but she would be taken anyway. Davey, I love you, but next time just refrain from telling me,' Will laughed as he gave Davey a hug. 'Catch you Monday?'

'Indeed you will, Will,' Davey laughed.

'Hilarious. See ya!' Will turned and walked out into the far more peaceful street. His anxiety immediately fading as he found space to breathe and could more easily distinguish between different sounds. Despite enjoying himself, for the most part, Will still arrived home annoyed that he couldn't continue on with his friends, that he found it so excruciating to remain at the bar the longer the evening went on.

Once again the familiar safety and calm of his sanctuary, and the words he was writing before him, felt like the only place he wanted to live.

Chapter Five

Jess

With Friday arriving, so did the blind date with Marie's mysterious friend. The excitement and giddiness which saw her agree to the date at the start of the week had slowly faded away as the working week drew to a close. What seemed like a good idea at the time—to take a chance and do something out of character—now had Jess dreading the end of the day.

Alas, the end of the day arrived and Jess was left with no more distractions before meeting up with Darren. Cait had taken it upon herself to accompany Jess home and help her get ready. In reality it was more to ensure that Jess didn't have a panic attack and spend the night under the covers with a book instead of meeting at the agreed time. It wasn't in Jess' nature to skip out on an agreed meetup—nor was it to agree to a blind date—so Cait wasn't going to leave it to chance.

'Okay Jess, what are we thinking dress-wise? And let's keep in mind that your usual work attire will not do for this outing,' Cait asked with a cheeky grin. She began flicking through items hanging in Jess' wardrobe, occasionally throwing one onto the bed.

'I guess we'll go with something similar to what I wore on Monday with some slight alterations?' Jess replied without a large amount of conviction, staring at herself in the mirror on the open wardrobe door.

'I like where your head's at Jess,' Cait agreed. 'Comfortable but sexy. Maybe we can make something out of this night after all.'

'What's that supposed to mean?' Jess played dumb, however she was well-aware of the shift in her mood.

'Girl, you've been getting so uptight today that I seriously considered whether you were already sabotaging it. You don't know this guy. He could be amazing. You heard Marie list off his credentials.'

'We have no basis that Marie's judgment is in any way in line with mine. It's not like she's an impartial third party here. He could just as easily be terrible.'

'Well you won't know until you meet him. A well timed joke, a touch of your hand, bodies close dancing, he lifts your chin and you'll be all his.'

Jess glared at her friend. 'That's not fair. Don't use my books against me. Anyway, that never happens in real life. Do you have any idea the odds of everything in the universe falling into place for that specific scenario to happen? Completely unrealistic.'

'And yet they seem to be your expectations,' Cait replied knowing she was entering dangerous territory.

'I definitely don't expect that. It's not my fault that everyone who talks to me is an arsehole. That's not a very high bar to get over.'

'You've got me there. Every drunk guy that approaches you at a bar, when you do go, is an arsehole. That is a factual statement.'

'Don't think I can't hear your tone, mum.'

'How dare you!' Cait exclaimed, hand on her chest and clutching her pearls in fake shock, causing Jess to laugh. 'Anyway, back to clothes. I'm thinking this sexy little tank. Jess, have you been holding out on me?' Cait pulled out a red tank top from Jess' wardrobe. 'Why is the tag still on?'

'Ummmm…because I've never worn it,' Jess sounded almost apologetic. 'Audrey got it for me once when I helped her with some wedding shopping. It isn't me.'

'It isn't you? You wear this and your chin won't be the only thing they're touching. You'll need some personal security. They're clothes, Jess. Your one true love will fall for your personality. There's nothing wrong with accessorising to open the doors a little.'

Jess glared, knowing exactly what Cait was insinuating. She snatched the top from Cait and threw it back in the wardrobe. 'This will be earned, not given.'

'Feisty. Let's keep up that intensity when you meet. He might be into it.'

Jess took out another t-shirt and held it in front of her.

Cait wasn't best pleased with the choice. 'Jess, nooooooo. Come on. This isn't first date appropriate.'

'Correct,' Jess agreed. 'This is blind date appropriate. It shows me and my personality. If he's a reader he'll find it funny. I'll even meet you halfway and wear this jacket over the top.' Jess picked out a cropped sage shirt-jacket with short sleeves.

'Fine. I can work with that. We'll swap out the sneakers for flats. Now…the hair,' Cait stood on her tip-toes and walked around Jess looking at the current state of her hair.

'What's wrong with my hair?'

'Nothing. Your hair's cute. Always is. Just thinking we can do a little more for the occasion,' Cait said, taking Jess' hair in her hands and moving to different positions as both looked on in the mirror. 'Let's go a loose braid. Shows off a bit of your personality but, more importantly, shows off a little neck.'

'That works for me. Let's get this done so I can get this over with,' Jess said with a sigh.

'Jess…you're all over the place right now and I'm gonna need a bit of positivity, okay? Work with me here please.'

Jess perked up her voice, albeit sarcastically, and repeated herself with a much improved level of bubbliness. 'Let's get this done so I can get this over with!'

'That's the spirit!' Cait laughed.

Jess arrived at The Green Vine a few minutes later than agreed as per request from Cait.

'Make him wait a little,' she had said while Jess was getting anxious over time. Given Cait was giving her a lift it was still in her hands when Jess would arrive.

Jess closed the car door and waved to Cait as she drove away before taking a minute to collect herself. *It's fine,* she told herself. *It's not like you had anything to do anyway. The books will still be there when you get home.*

A deep breath completed Jess' mental preparation before she began walking to the entrance having no idea what she was looking for. Jess had been insistent that she choose the venue to allow her the home ground advantage. Having knowledge of exits, facilities and security locations set her mind somewhat at ease should the date go sideways. Security was clearly doing their job as they were escorting a few highly intoxicated patrons out of the venue.

'Jess?' came a voice behind her.

She turned around to be pleasantly surprised by the man standing before her. She inwardly praised Marie for the first of her descriptions being spot on.

'Yes,' she replied—a small smile escaping the corners of her mouth. 'Darren, I presume?'

Darren was a very well groomed man, freshly cut and shaved to a thin beard. He was tall with dark skin and despite being thin he did seem quite toned based on the contours seen through his tight black shirt beneath an open black leather jacket—an item of clothing Jess was sure he'd regret very quickly given the warming summer weather. Black boots sat beneath his slim jeans with his extending hand bringing Jess' gaze back up from his legs.

'Yes, very nice to meet you.'

'And you,' Jess daintily shook his hand.

Upon letting go of her hand Darren immediately shifted her jacket, reading the print on Jess' shirt. 'I left my boyfriend in my other books. Funny,' he approved with a smile.

'Thanks. Shall we head in?'

'After you,' Darren said motioning toward the entrance.

As they began walking in Jess removed her jacket, no longer needing to hide her shirt. It became clear very quickly that the choice of venue was not the best idea. The Green Vine was as packed—and loud—as Jess had ever seen it. She had completely forgotten about all the Christmas functions that would be happening at just over a week out from Christmas. Whereas the usual crowd would just be getting going, the state of a vast number of people suggested they were already a number of hours in—some clumsily bumping into her as they made their way out and presumably to the next stop in their evening.

Jess turned to Darren. 'Sorry. It's not usually like this.' A near shout was required for her voice to be accurately heard.

'It's okay. I'm sure we'll manage,' Darren replied.

Easy for him to say. He towered above most whereas Jess had to make do with a lot of sweaty necks. As far as Jess was concerned a date was meant for getting to know someone and she couldn't imagine that being possible the way it was.

Slowly they managed to weave their way to the bar where at least Darren was kind enough to buy Jess a glass of white wine—as well as one for himself. Darren kept hold of both glasses as they managed to find a corner where they could at least stand and place their glasses on a plank atop a retaining wall—although they almost lost them, having been bumped into a table, resulting in Jess apologising profusely to the four sitting there shouting a conversation.

As far as Jess was concerned, the date was going terribly, although the one saving grace was that it wasn't due to the company. After a few false starts at each trying to begin a conversation—only to be drowned out by the noise—Darren noticed that the ropes and small fences were being cleared from the function areas. They scurried as quickly as they could to get a small table at the far end of the venue. Along with having another bar open to everyone—and a general thinning of the mass of people— Jess and Darren could finally sit and converse at a near normal level. Her hopes began to rise as fortune was turning her way.

'I can't believe I didn't consider how busy it would be here,' Jess said, again apologising.

'I'm sure it was just as busy everywhere else—and if it wasn't then it's probably somewhere we wouldn't have wanted to go anyway.'

'I guess you're right. Are you always so glass half full?' she asked, his stock rising in her estimations.

'I have to be given how I live,' he replied.

'You own a café, right? I assume that's pretty risky?'

'It is if you don't know what you're doing—or know the right time to get out. One of the advantages is that I don't get the insanely packed drunk hordes bearing down on me. On the flip side the revenue they'll take in tonight will be insane. Marie tells me you work at the library and do a lot of work with kids? That's great.'

'Thanks. Yes I do. It's very rewarding.' Jess' mood was improving the more they spoke, allowing her to relax and maybe even enjoy herself should it continue.

'Even if Marie hadn't told me, your t-shirt speaks volumes about your personality.'

'And what does it say?' she asked playfully, almost thrusting out her chest to show off her shirt.

'Firstly, that you clearly love books—and romantic ones at that. Secondly, that you're clear-headed in what you like and aren't ashamed of it. You won't hide who you are and if people aren't on board then you don't need them around you.'

'Very observant, Darren. Is that something you subscribe to?' she asked, trying to get a reading on the type of person Darren was.

'It's a trait I respect a lot,' he answered—much to Jess' approval. 'I wish more people were like that. Just upfront with who they are and people can take it or leave it. My parents are stuck in a time where everything has to be a certain way. There's not a lot of room for negotiation or understanding.'

'Are they good with you owning a café?' Jess asked, knowing how harsh parents could be on choices of occupation.

'They are now. It took a long time though. Once they finally realised how seriously I took the business side, they got on board with it. I've owned six cafés in the past. Built them up and then sold them off. Once my parents understood that I wasn't just sinking money into a hobby, they conveniently forgot how they behaved at the start of the journey.' Darren laughed allowing Jess to join and continue to build the rapport between them. 'I ended up getting a degree in business studying part time. I love learning about it and keeping on top of everything that's happening in the industry.'

Jess took a slight pause to run through Marie's list of attributes in her head. 'Marie mentioned you love to read. How do you find the time while running a business and keeping on top of business-y type things?'

'Marie said I love to read? I guess she did regularly see me with my head in books. They would have been part of my studying and the continuation of my learning after I graduated,' he answered in the most disappointing fashion as far as Jess was concerned.

'So you're not really into your fiction stories then?' she asked, giving Darren one more chance at redemption.

'Not really. I mean I'm interested when people tell me about the stories they enjoy, but I don't really have any time for them myself.'

This was concerning to Jess. Technically Marie didn't lie. He read all the time, owned a café and was really hot. Jess assumed he knew his way around a coffee machine and a kitchen. *I guess taking an interest in the stories that I love can be half a point,* she thought to herself. *A guy who ticks a lot of the boxes and appreciates that I'm good with kids is definitely setting the highest standard so far. Maybe I can see where this goes after all?*

Jess decided that she should at least give him the night to see if there was any possibility that anything could work. She was already out so what was the harm in getting to know Darren more.

Jess and Darren spent the next hour on a couple more drinks each while swapping stories about their travels, families and a few anecdotes concerning Marie. All things considered Jess thought this to be one of the most enjoyable dates she'd ever been on.

'Want to go have a dance?' Darren asked.

'Sure,' Jess replied. 'It looks like a lot of the early starters have left so it should be a much more accommodating crowd now.' She smiled as she stood and they made their way back to the other side of her usual bar to get to the dance floor.

Jess had to admit that Darren was a very good dancer. So much so that he even managed to get those around them to lift their game. *Alright,* Jess thought. *He's definitely the life of the party in the most positive of ways. That's a tick in the pros column.* She spent their time dancing with a smile on her face, often laughing as Darren managed to get the most timid of patrons to move their hips with a respectable level of competence.

'I'm going to go to the ladies room and get another drink. Do you want anything?' Jess asked.

'Come and get me when you're done and we can grab a fresh drink and sit down?' he responded—clearly still feeling the music through his body.

'Sounds good. See you soon.'

Jess walked to the ladies room in a jubilant mood. She retrieved her phone from her purse, eager to give Cait an update on how well the night was going. Not even a near miss with a drunken spill of a drink could dampen her mood.

After relieving herself and a quick makeup refresh she returned to the dance floor to retrieve her date and get another drink. Darren was still full of energy as she watched and giggled on her short journey over to him—although a short ginger man getting a little handsy with him did almost get her jealousy going. *Calm down mate. He's with me,* she thought to herself, suddenly realising just how well the date was going.

Jess retrieved her man and they sat down with a fresh drink. She had another wine whereas Darren had some concoction of different beverages that she couldn't quite keep track of.

'I'm having a great time,' Darren said, still bobbing his head to the music.

'So am I,' said Jess, smiling. 'To be honest I was really worried about coming out tonight. I don't date often, especially blind dates.'

'Excuse me?' he asked and leaned in a little. It seemed all the time on the dance floor had affected his hearing.

'I said I don't date often, especially blind dates,' Jess laughed at having to speak up.

Darren's face suddenly dropped as a sense of dread toiled in the pit of Jess' stomach.

'Did you say blind date?' Darren asked, his brows lowering and jaw tensing. 'I could kill Marie. I'm sorry, Jess. She didn't say anything about a date. She told me she wanted me to go out with you tonight because you don't get out often. I guess I should've read between the lines. One last attempt at getting me back in line.'

Jess was speechless. The wheels turning as she recounted all the conversations of the night. The lump in her throat making it near impossible to say anything as she suddenly clicked on all the signs she had missed.

'Your respect for my authenticity,' Jess managed to squeeze out. 'It wasn't about your work was it?'

'No. I'm sorry, Jess. I honestly thought you knew. I never imagined Marie would do something like this. I know she's pretty set in her beliefs but this is beyond disgraceful.'

Darren reached out to place his hand on Jess'. She recoiled slightly before allowing his sympathetic gesture, knowing her humiliation wasn't his doing.

'I feel like such an idiot,' she said as tears began to fall down her cheeks.

'Please don't, Jess. You've got nothing to be ashamed of. We were both tricked by an ignorant bigot. She won't get away with this, don't you worry about that.'

'Oh, I know she won't. I'm working somewhere else on Monday afternoon but as soon as I tell Cait, she'll regret she even met us.' Jess awkwardly laughed picturing what Cait would do to Marie once she saw her. 'I guess I should go home,' Jess said as she stood up from the table.

'Are you sure? Just because things haven't turned out like you thought, it doesn't mean we can't still have a fun night.'

Jess appreciated how caring Darren was being considering how angry he must have been. 'That's okay. My boyfriend awaits,' Jess said, awkwardly laughing and pointing at her shirt. 'And it looks like you've got an admirer awaiting you.' Jess nodded back to the dance floor where the ginger man kept glancing in their direction while dancing with his friends.

'Okay. Well please take my number and let me know when you get home safe. We can keep each other posted on how we take vengeance.'

Jess burst out laughing with a snort. She appreciated the sentiment that wouldn't be out of place in the stories she loved.

After exchanging phone numbers, Darren gave Jess a long and caring hug. 'I honestly have had a great time tonight,' he said. 'Come down to the café some time and I'll whip up something nice for you. Any time you're looking for another fun night just give me a call.'

'Thank you, Darren. You really are an amazing guy. If that little ginge does anything to upset you let me know and I'll rip his throat out.' They both laughed.

'Thanks, Jess. And you're an amazing woman. You'll find your prince.'

Jess left The Green Vine and immediately burst into tears.

Taking out her phone she called Cait who wasted no time picking her up and taking her home. Cait spent the night with Jess taking in the insanely devious plot Marie had constructed and how she used Jess for her bigotry. Eventually Jess managed to fall asleep, exhausted from crying.

Chapter Six

Jess

Jess woke up on Saturday with a headache. On top of the number of beverages she had consumed she was dehydrated from a night of flowing tears. Jess was angry at herself for letting her guard down, going against her better judgment and allowing herself to be used by Marie simply because she wouldn't accept Darren for who he was. Not only did she feel betrayed by Marie, she felt betrayed by herself. Jess knew better than to let others dictate who she should see and when. Leaving herself open to thoughts of *what if* futures for a prospect that never was. The lesson had been well and truly learned.

Cait felt the brunt of Jess' shortness that morning, however was happy to take it feeling somewhat responsible for ensuring Jess had both attended the faux-date, and lowering her guard. She also felt great sympathy for Jess' terrible luck. While making Jess some breakfast Cait had tried to lighten the mood with a joke.

'What are the odds of that, hey?' she had joked, while poaching some eggs in a pot.

Rather than reply, Jess glared daggers at her friend while holding her head up, resting her chin on her palm at the kitchen bench.

'Yeah, that wasn't my best work. Sorry, Jess. I just can't believe that happened. Marie's always bee-'

'Don't say her name,' Jess snapped.

'Fair enough,' Cait complied, glad to be able to keep her eyes on the eggs.

'Sorry, Cait. It's not your fault.'

'The deception, no. But I made sure you didn't back out. And helped make you oh so sexy,' Cait turned and Blue Steeled in Jess' direction, making her finally giggle.

'You were just helping…and I did look good, didn't I.' Both women laughed. 'Just don't mention she-who-shall-not-be-named.'

'At least you won't have to see her on Monday but trust me, she will be dealt with. It's just unfortunate for the kids. They don't deserve that. Hopefully they don't grow up thinking the same as her.' Cait waved a spatula around the kitchen—Jess having to dodge a stray drop of oil. At least a gourmet breakfast may help slightly.

'I'm sure one day I'll see her again and I don't know what I'll do when it happens,' Jess groaned as she dropped her face into her hands.

'Chances are that will be a next year problem.'

'Oh cool, so knowing my luck, guaranteed to see her this week then?' Jess said, pulling down at her cheeks.

Cait walked to the kitchen bench and laid the eggs on toast before drizzling some hollandaise over the top. 'You couldn't possibly have that much bad luck. It must be all used up now.'

'Please don't jinx it.' Jess pulled over a plate and—not caring for cutlery in her current state—picked up her breakfast and proceeded to force as much as possible into her mouth. 'If I've learned anything it can always get worse,' Jess mumbled, mouth full.

Cait walked around the bench and put her arms around Jess' shoulders. 'I promise from now on I'll let you decide your fate. Whatever you want to do is good with me…as long as you keep letting me dress you for dates.' Cait kissed Jess on the cheek and laughed.

As the day progressed, Jess moped around her house less and less. She even managed to warm up some leftover food after Cait had left. Cait had a second date with the *Spanish mixologist* as Cait had described him. As much as the thought of dates made her queasy, she was still happy for Cait being excited about her new man.

Jess turned down breakfast at her parents' on Sunday morning —the thought of giddy wedding planning flaring her frustrations. She claimed a small cold as being responsible and didn't want to make anyone sick so close to the holidays. Having been completely unproductive on Saturday, the weekend chores had to be compressed into Sunday. Jess chose to think of it as an opportunity to take her mind off everything and fire up some epic fantasy audiobooks—specifically without romance. It did the trick and Jess ended the weekend feeling a little more like herself.

With a week remaining of work until Christmas, Jess was desperate for it to be as uneventful as possible. Monday morning was spent in relative silence. Cait didn't want to share how her love-life was progressing and, given recent events, Jess didn't want to know. There was no awkwardness between them, it just wasn't a topic they cared to broach, choosing to talk about the weekend's books and joke around about anything else—other than Marie.

Jess was concerned with her afternoon filling in at a library she was unfamiliar with—a brief tour to come upon arrival.

Cait accommodated the blacklist of topics by asking questions around the activities Jess had planned for the afternoon—catching herself every time she started to joke about outlandish ideas she had for dealing with Marie.

With the morning over Jess decided to leave and eat her lunch elsewhere—in new surroundings—to avoid any possible oncoming tension for the afternoon. Given she had an afternoon with children—and desiring a return to the familiar—Jess had dressed for the day in a black, drawstring, full length, high-waisted bow dress above a white, butterfly-sleeve blouse. Really wanting to embrace a tavern look. Her red flats were complemented by her giant red butterfly claw clip—half up—and red lipstick.

Upon arriving at the alternate place of work she noticed a grassed area at the front, shaded by trees. Since the day was relatively cool, Jess let it be known she had arrived before taking her lunch out to the grass to enjoy some peaceful nature. Despite the nearby path she was yet to see anyone in the area as she walked out to sit on the grass. A simple sandwich and grapes were on the menu with the chirping of birds providing a perfect ambiance to prepare Jess for the afternoon.

It wasn't long, however, before her solitude was interrupted. Although momentarily, it left a lasting impression.

Will

Friday evening had been about all the social interaction Will could handle with the rest of the weekend spent recharging his batteries —not that he ever needed much arm-twisting to live the solitary life. The chaotic and unpredictable variables that are people weren't conducive with his anxiety levels, especially knowing what the final week of work had in store for him. He used the opportunity to make more progress than expected with his writing and get in a good, relaxing read at the park with an iced latte.

Monday morning started with the same routine as most days— he and Davey visiting Torah for their morning coffee before taking on the day. This particular Monday was the pre-Christmas present that neither of them wanted. The entire morning was blocked out for a particularly difficult client—Shenae—who couldn't choose between delegating and micro-managing her projects, so decided on delegating until the last minute with unrealistic and immovable deadlines.

'We don't get paid enough for this,' moaned Davey, standing outside the front door to the office and refusing to enter. 'It'd be totally fine if I just left, right? Just walked away and began life anew someplace else?'

'I guess you could but your bag is still in there,' Will responded.

'I'm prepared to sacrifice it. Who needs bags and things anyway?'

'Or keys,' Will added smirking.

'Ahhhhhhhh dammit! It's okay. I'm sure I can pick the lock to my place. How hard could it be?' Davey continued to live in hope.

'Hard enough for people to make a career of it and charge a pretty penny.'

'So you're saying it's possible?'

'Don't leave me,' Will said as they both laughed.

'Fine. Let's get this over with. Then I'm off site for another meeting after a quick lunch before a networking event tonight. Yay for me!'

'Yay indeed.'

Both walked into the office with full expectation of spending the morning being repeatedly told how they got everything wrong while having to keep positive.

Half an hour later Shenae entered—with an entourage of employees she had apparently delegated the work to—in order to get to the bottom of how Davey, Will and Aisha *misunderstood the brief* despite sign-offs at every step of the journey. Will had been dragged in for his technical knowledge and having written a spec based on all the information they were given. Aisha was already part-way through her designs having received wireframe and concept sign-off.

The meeting kicked off in brutal fashion. Shenae's aggression was in full flow before everyone had even taken a seat in the boardroom. Will, Davey and Aisha were all seething inside. This wasn't the first time this had happened, however they were always under strict instructions to keep this particular client from cancelling their highly valuable, long-term contract.

Davey's attempt to calm the situation and explain the current status of the project fell on deaf ears, despite producing the receipts in the form of email chains showing where Shenae had delegated sign-off authority to Melissa—who they were then informed was no longer on the project as she was no longer employed. That then set off Shenae on a tirade of insults of the work they had already done —pushing Aisha to the verge of tears.

Will had heard enough. The rage coursing through him had become overwhelming and he could no longer keep it contained. They had all been the punching bag for too long and where Will would have frozen in the past, he wasn't going to let his friends continue to be disrespected. Will closed his eyes for a few seconds to centre himself.

While aggressive in tone, Will's push back in the defence of his friends was still rather measured—sticking to the facts and pointing out that both sides had won awards based on the work they had done. Where he began to stray too far was to also point out Shenae's repeated process of delegating and then taking over projects—resulting in drastic changes to projects.

The door to the boardroom opened and the general manager—Rob—stepped inside the room. Will knew this was it. Having spent so long helping grow the business he was about to spend Christmas finding a new job. *At least Davey and Aisha will be okay*, he thought knowing they had nothing to answer for.

'Shenae, could I have a word in my office please,' he said, immediately turning and walking out of the room. Shenae stood and followed.

An awkward silence filled the room as everyone tried to process what had happened and what was currently happening.

'I think your designs were great,' one of the women in the entourage said with a smile. A murmur of agreement floated by the others.

'Thanks,' Aisha managed to squeak out.

The boardroom door opened again. Shenae took her seat as Davey, Will and Aisha were summoned. Entering Rob's office he took a seat at his desk as the three employees stood. Given only one chair was available they all decided to just ignore its existence.

'Okay. Where do I start?' Rob began as Will's heart beat at a ferocious pace. 'I know Shenae is a handful and I also know what I've said in the past about keeping her onside. What you don't know is that I had a conversation with Shenae when she had her initial blowup and took over the project, where I gave her parameters about how the meeting will run. I was listening to her tirade when she walked in and, to be perfectly honest, I was disgusted by what she said. I know how much grief she gives you but she is our biggest client. I just reminded Shenae about what we had previously discussed so the rest of the meeting will be going over what's there and what she wants changed. Don't give her any numbers at the moment—we'll sort that after. That's all. Will just a quick word. You two can get back to the boardroom.'

For the briefest of moments Will had thought he'd managed to escape, however now being alone brought all the fears back for him.

'Will,' Rob said, leaving it hanging for a few moments. 'That was a little intense, yeah? You know you can't talk to clients like that.'

'I know. Sorry, I just snapped. We work so hard and she keeps doing this to us,' Will answered, eyes downcast.

'I get how she is. Unfortunately-' Will's throat seized up knowing what was coming. 'I have to give you a written warning even though you were factually correct. I'll need you to apologise to her when you get back in there.'

A wave of relief washed over Will as it hit him that he didn't have to find a new job. 'I understand. Won't happen again.'

'Good to hear. That'll be all, Will,' Rob put his head down and began reading whatever was on his desk—a cue for Will to leave.

Will left the office and couldn't help but smile. Despite officially being in a worse position than when he started the day, at least he was still employed.

The rest of the meeting went relatively smoothly—especially in comparison to how it began. After swallowing his pride and apologising—only receiving a nod in return—they went through all the changes to the requirements, wireframes and concepts. In the end not a lot was changed as Will and Aisha justified their decisions—justifications Shenae would have received from Melissa had she talked to her.

After Shenae and her entourage had left the office Will was finally able to take his lunch break—a little later than he usually would. Despite still being annoyed at their treatment he was relieved it was over and he could take a walk to clear his head.

With his lunch complete, Will left the office and took his usual route around the nearby park and recreation center. The route he had perfected over the last couple of years ensured he'd come into contact with the least amount of people as possible to maximise the mental health boost he would gain from it. The last thing he needed was a group of people taking up the width of the path while having a needlessly loud conversation.

Will rounded the bend and continued walking down the winding path along the library. As he reached the crest of a small hill he saw a woman sitting beneath a tree eating grapes. What was initially striking to him was the way she was dressed. *She looks like she's been pulled straight out of one of my books,* he thought to himself.

Will was instantly captivated as rays of sun breached through the leaves of the tree to light her perfect blonde hair—the large red clip striking against the fairness of both her hair and skin. Her chin slightly tilted up and her eyes closed as she took in the warmth of the sun on her skin.

As the path wound closer to this ethereal woman, Will accidentally ruined the tranquility by stepping on a dead leaf—the crunch slightly startling the woman and making her turn to look in his direction. He cursed himself for breaking her peace, although any hint of annoyance failed to materialise from her as she smiled at him. Her brown eyes and red lips kept Will transfixed in a moment of peaceful exuberance—making his heart skip a beat and stomach jump. A warmth flowed through him that he hadn't felt for many years—and wasn't sure he'd ever feel again until this moment.

Will uncontrollably smiled back at her with all the warmth that had built beyond the containment of his body. If he had the ability to stop time he would have stayed in that moment forever. He had no desire for any other existence. Being one whose life was usually ruled by logic, Will was lost in surrendering to his emotions and never wanted to leave.

The moment, however, was just a moment and as he roused from his daze, Will suddenly found that his body had taken him beyond the woman, continuing down the path, past the library. His mind had exploded into a network of possibilities of what could be —most a beautifully crafted romance, the odd one a nightmare of humiliation. It was an inspiration of storytelling he'd only ever felt in the darkest of times. He then realised that those possibilities could only come from a single origin—talking to the woman he had seen peacefully sitting on the grass. But as Will had a habit of doing, he had gotten distracted by the worlds created in his head and kept walking. The opportunity gone—and with it any possible story of blissful happiness.

Jess

Jess was enjoying the warmth of the sun on her face as the breeze swayed the leaves and branches of the tree—allowing momentary rays to catch her. The birds, clean air, and peaceful moments she rarely had outside of her home was exactly what she needed to arrest the downward slide of recent days. She revelled in the moment knowing that she'd soon have to return to the library to begin her afternoon's work.

A crunch interrupted her peace, jolting her back to reality. She turned to see what had caused the disturbance. The crunch a result of dead leaves on the nearby path, stepped on by a man walking by. His smart-casual attire of black t-shirt and jeans over boots made Jess take notice—the glasses an added bonus. He looked to her like a man that took care of himself without being obsessed. A simple, nicely styled haircut and well-groomed short—almost stubble—beard showing the beginnings of grey offering a wisdom many didn't possess.

Jess could see in his eyes how it almost hurt him that he had disturbed her—a show of empathy that sent a jolt through her heart. She began to imagine the kindness a man like this could possess and it brought a warm smile to her face.

The smile he returned was almost enough to make her weep as his eyes relaxed to show the kindness she was longing for. A strength, yet affection that could only come from one whose entire world was yours.

Jess held his gaze for as far as her neck would turn before breaking it. In the time she had turned her body the man had continued walking beyond her and out of her life. She briefly attempted to call out for him to return, however the emotion of the moment caused her voice to fail and he was gone.

Jess finished her lunch slowly—choosing to revel in the feeling he had given her momentarily and dreaming of possibilities that never came to pass. An honourable knight, perhaps, come to whisk her away.

After milking the lunch break as much as she could Jess stood to return to work—taking a path back to the library. As she neared the entrance she felt a pull to turn back in hope, just to see. As she reached the door she saw the man again—returning the same way he had come—past the tree under which she sat when he had briefly stolen her heart. *Has he returned to see me again?* Jess thought to herself. Part of her yearned to run after him and explore that possibility. The other part knew there were children waiting for her in the library. With a dejected sigh she turned and walked through the door.

Chapter Seven

Jess

Jess couldn't help but call Cait the second she got home to update her on what had happened that day.

'Noooooo!' was Cait's initial response.

'Yes,' was all Jess could reply with.

'Noooooo!' Cait repeated.

'Still yes.'

'But…noooooo! Jess, you get uptight when you see a man look in your direction. There's no way you could fall for some random guy walking past. Just…noooooo!' Cait began to uncontrollably laugh.

'I'm glad I can provide you with some entertainment,' Jess

managed to contain herself for a few moments before she also broke into laughter, knowing how ridiculous the story sounded.

Jess realised that working at that particular library was a once off that afternoon. She cursed herself that she'd missed her opportunity.

'And now I screwed it all up by not saying anything. I have no idea who he is.'

'It's not all lost,' Cait attempted to raise Jess' hopes. 'Maybe during lunch tomorrow we do a drive-by and catch him on another walk?'

'Thanks Cait but the chances are pretty low. We're relying on the fact that he's always in the area; always goes for a walk on that exact route; and that I'm not going insane in what I think I saw. He probably thought I was some crazy woman out of the asylum for the afternoon.'

'Maybe he likes a little crazy with his hot?'

'You're right. I am going insane. I've let those perfect romances in my books get into my head,' Jess' mood had taken a swift turn from when she initially told Cait her exciting news.

'First, I was joking. You're not insane. Second, we have no idea what he thought. You might be completely right. Maybe he finds that attire super sexy and his mind exploded the second he saw you. Won't know until you talk to him.'

'Which we can't do. Yay.' Jess' dispirited sarcasm had taken the reigns.

'Chin up, Jess. We'll work something out. And if not, maybe you at least have an idea of what you're looking for. Apparently it's not that bad-boy you were supposed to change.'

Jess laughed. 'Maybe you're right. Maybe I should leave that for the books and really I want a nice, caring guy I can snuggle with.'

'That's the spirit!' Cait yelled. 'Let's do that drive-by tomorrow. Maybe you'll get lucky and he's there again. Like it was meant to be and the universe is pulling you two together.'

'I hope you're right, Cait.'

Will

The afternoon wasn't overly productive for Will. The events from his lunch break were tumbling around his head—each new iteration sparking off a networked series of events with differing outcomes. On the one hand it was exciting to have this creativity flowing through him—full of possibilities and hope. On the other, the constant explosion of thought—especially when potentially painful outcomes surfaced—often caused him to freeze and miss opportunities that came his way.

Will needed an outlet to process all of this, however with Davey out of the office for the remainder of the day all he could do was try to get through while keeping the whirlwind of emotions from overwhelming him. Once at home he could either find an outlet or a distraction to calm his mind. Knowing that Davey wasn't reachable until the next day Will did the one thing he knew would process his thoughts best. He would write.

The night was restless for Will. The overstimulation couldn't be curtailed enough to fall asleep for extended periods. Even when he did, his mind continued to spark narratives in his dreams—some easily forgotten, some staying with him.

Will rose before his morning alarm, seeing no point in continuing to try and get any more sleep. Coffee was a requirement before he even considered getting ready for work. He needed to make sure he was coherent when he spoke to Davey so he jotted down some notes into his phone to make sure he didn't miss any key points and ruin the timeline. Despite the event being etched into his brain, Will was prone to jumping around during a story when telling it in person.

The process was slow and arduous, however Will managed to get himself to work on time. Davey appeared a little worse for wear after the networking event the previous evening. It was no wonder he was always dragged into the events despite the lack of seniority within the company—Davey was the life of the party after all.

Will waited out the front of the office for Davey to arrive. Despite the lack of sleep he was still giddy over the chance—almost—meeting with the woman and was itching the fill Davey in.

'Davey! You'll never belie-'

'Stop! Lower the volume, please…and the pace. Maybe coffee first,' Davey groaned.

'Event went well?' Will asked, bouncing on the spot with a massive grin on his face.

Davey looked Will up and down. 'If you needed to take a piss maybe you should've gone before you left the office. I'm not turning the car around once we're headed for coffee.'

'I don't need to piss, Davey. I've got something really important I need to tell you.'

'Ugh. Can it wait a minute? Your vibe right now is a lot,' Davey waved his hand in Will's general area.

'I can wait,' Will said, although still bursting at the seams. 'I've got notes.'

'Notes? You picking up an award I didn't know about? Doubtful after everything that happened yesterday.'

'Well, Davey me boy, you only know what happened for half of yesterday. Anyway, tell me about your successful networking so I can get onto my news.'

'Ok… You're acting super weird, just so you know.'

'I know,' Will agreed.

'So the event went well. We might have some pretty big leads and partnerships in the near future if all comes off. I really need this Christmas break though. It's definitely taking its toll.'

Davey spent the few minutes walking to the coffee shop listing all the big-wigs he'd been schmoozing the previous night, while adding little nuggets of gossip he'd managed to coax out of them along the way.

They reached their sanctuary and ordered their usual with Torah. Small talk was short as she noticed the odd state of both of them and thought it better to leave questions for the next day.

'Okay,' Davey harshly exhaled before straightening and putting on his best fake smile. 'Let's hear this amazing news you have.'

Will was in such a state he didn't even care about the slightly condescending tone. He didn't have time to let that get in the way.

'So I met a girl yesterday…well didn't actually meet…more like walked by-'

'I'm going to stop you there for a second, Will. Take a breath and maybe get those notes out you were talking about. I am intrigued though. My boy's all flustered.'

Will took a deep breath as he retrieved his phone from his pocket. 'Ok. From the start. After you left for your meeting I had lunch and went for my usual walk. When I reached the top of the hill, near the library, I saw a woman serenely enjoying her lunch on the grass. She was sooooo beautiful, Davey. Like, fantasy princess beautiful. As in she was even dressed like she came straight out of a fantasy book. I couldn't believe it. So I was walking on the path near her and stepped on a stupid dead leaf which completely ruined her tranquil state. She looked at me and then smiled. The most perfect smile. Then I smiled back and it was like we were connected on some cosmic level.'

In the excitement of the storytelling Davey's smile became sincere. This was exactly the tonic he needed to get his day going. Even Torah had stopped making their coffees to lean out of the window and listen. Both were heavily invested.

Will continued his story. 'That feeling in my heart and stomach. The warm and fuzzies flowing through me. I haven't felt that in years.'

'Oh my god, Will. This gives me life!' Davey was now matching Will's excitement.

'And then I continued on my walk and haven't been able to stop thinking about her since! My brain hasn't stopped. I couldn't sleep. She was perfect, Davey.'

'You skipped a bit. You talked to her right? What's her name?' Davey's smile was beginning to wane—fearing that he already knew the answer.

Will stared back at him blankly—his own smile beginning to fade.

'You got her number, right Will?'

'I-' was all Will could muster—the enthusiasm now completely gone.

'You...' Davey awkwardly giggled. 'You got her number... Will...you got it, right?... And her name?... You got all her details, right? Coz you talked to her...right?'

Will said nothing, his face distraught now that he could no longer ride the wave of excitement to cover what he already knew was a monumental mistake.

Davey punched Will in the shoulder. 'Will!'

Torah left the window, returning to make their coffees, laughing at the damp squib of a story she'd just been subjected to. 'Will, you grade-A dumbass. HAHAHA!'

'Not helping, Torah!' Davey shouted at her—passers-by

shocked by his sudden outburst. 'Will, why didn't you talk to her?'

'I don't know, Davey. The same reason I never talk to anyone. I just froze mentally. I was so transfixed by her that my body kept walking on autopilot.'

'We both know that's not entirely the reason, Will. Perchance was your brain running through everything that could possibly go wrong if you had talked to her?'

Will lowered his gaze to his feet. 'Yeah, maybe some of those scenarios popped up too… I hate myself, Davey. What am I going to do? She was amazing and I don't have anything to go off.'

'First, let's drop that negative talk. We're going to figure this out. Maybe she'll be out again today for lunch and you can get a second try.'

'Yeah, maybe.' Will was dejected—in stark contrast to his mood when he had started the story.

Torah called up Davey and Will to collect their coffees. Handing them over she looked at Will again and burst into laughter. 'Awww. I'm sorry, Will. It just started so well and fell off a cliff.'

'Torah,' Davey leaned into the window. 'You want to keep seeing these pretty faces every morning you better check that attitude. We need all hands on deck!… Love youuuuuu.'

'I'm sorry, Will. I really hope you find this girl,' Torah apologised, still trying to stifle a giggle.

Will simply turned away and walked back to the office—so dejected that he nearly walked across the road without seeing the traffic.

'Let's not go that far, Will,' Davey grimaced as he pulled Will back.

Will constantly glanced at the clock all morning until lunch when he could retrace his steps in the hopes that she was there again. The time came and he raced out the door. As he crested the hill, Will slowed down, not seeing anybody around. *If I'm slow I'll get more time*, he thought. Will slowed to a very casual stroll by the time he had reached the path to the library. Seeing nobody in any direction, the fear began to rise that he had missed his chance. *I'll finish my loop and hope she's here when I come back around*, Will tried to convince himself.

In contrast to the previous day his mind was completely filled with every version of a worst-case scenario that he could possibly conjure up. The bubbling of fear became more intense as Will continued his walk for a further fifteen minutes—only to return to another empty patch of grass under the tree.

'Another conquest in the art of idiocy,' Will admonished himself —clenching his fists in anger at himself until his nails began to cut into his palms.

Will stopped briefly, looked up and took a deep breath— allowing him to release the tension in his hands before any real damage was done. *Maybe tomorrow*, he thought as he returned to the office. Walking upstairs Davey looked at him expectantly from his desk. Will simply shook his head and sat down hoping work could provide a distraction for the rest of the day.

Jess

Jess and Cait spent the next morning plotting their route around the area of the encounter, making sure that their timings matched when she had gone out for lunch. They figured they'd have enough time in their break for a few laps before having to drive back.

While Cait was giddy with excitement for the adventure they were embarking on, Jess was apprehensive that it would all end in disappointment. A feeling of annoyance around this area of her life was the norm, however this was something entirely new. Despite telling herself she was being stupid, she felt there was so much riding on this and it would end either in bliss or heartbreak.

The lunch break rolled around and Jess joined Cait in her car to drive her around while she kept a keen eye out in hope of seeing this man who was, in all ways, a complete stranger. Jess was quiet —her nervous energy making even Cait struggle to find anything to say. She fiddled nervously with her fingers in her lap with her head kept down until they approached the library.

'Okay, Jess. You keep looking around and I'll go as slow as I possibly can. Let me know if you see anything.'

'Okay,' Jess said, not inspiring any confidence of success in their mission.

The first lap brought no success. Very few people were even out walking, most likely due to the warmer weather. It only took them five minutes to complete the lap in the car. Two more laps brought no increase in activity.

'Let's stop in the library carpark for a little bit,' Jess suggested. 'We can eat our lunch and look around in case he walks by. If not we'll do a few more laps and head back.'

'Great idea, Jess. Hold on... I see somebody up front on the path. Maybe that's him?'

Cait slowed the car down so they could take a good look. 'This is slightly stalkery,' Cait added.

'I don't think that's him, Cait. Wrong body shape, no glasses. Now that we're getting closer he doesn't have any facial hair at all.'

'Maybe he shaved last night?'

'Nah. It's not him.'

Cait and Jess were suddenly shocked when a car behind beeped their horn.

'Just go around!' Cait shouted out her window. 'Asshole! Let's pull into the carpark and have lunch.'

They parked the car and ate their lunch with the air conditioner still running. Jess didn't finish her sandwich having lost her appetite with the losing battle in their search.

'I'm going to take a quick walk up the path and back. Just in case,' Jess said, opening the door.

Her short walk reaped no results despite lingering for an awkward amount of time at the top of the path. A few people walked past eyeing her strangely as she stood looking up and down the intersecting path.

Jess returned to Cait looking defeated.

'Still nothing?' Cait asked.

'Nope…nothing,' Jess responded.

'Okay. A couple more laps and we'll head back.'

They drove out of the carpark and completed two more laps before heading back to work. Nobody even remotely looked like her mystery man.

Turning off the car Jess simply sat looking down—tears beginning to well in the corners of her eyes.

'Are you okay?' Cait asked, placing a hand on her forearm.

Jess replied while attempting to hold back the choking feeling in her throat. 'Why am I being like this? This is so stupid. I saw this guy for a few seconds. We didn't speak. We both just smiled like a couple of idiots—at least I did. Maybe I saw from him what I wanted to and it never even happened. Now I'm sitting here in a ridiculous state like I've just been through a breakup.'

'It's okay to feel, Jess. You had a deep moment of connection. You didn't make that up. You had hope of something special. You dared to dream a little. You can't beat yourself up over that. Come on. Let's get back inside. You can let the kids cheer you up.'

Defeated, Jess unbuckled her seatbelt and opened the door, feeling broken again—much like she had over the weekend—

although this time with the feeling that she had lost something deep inside her.

Chapter Eight

Will

The final week of work before the Christmas break was a slog for Will and Davey. The last minute alterations and campaigns were coming thick and fast on top of an already overloaded schedule.

Despite the burnout that was exponentially building, Will was actually somewhat relieved to have the workload prevent his mind from wandering to places he really didn't want it to venture. Each day he walked the same path, hoping to get even the briefest glimpse of the woman who had refused to leave his dreams—and each day he returned to the office disappointed that she didn't appear.

Friday came and went. Close of business bringing a mix of

cheers and exhausted sighs—along with a few bottles of bubbles, wine and beer. Will slumped in his chair, happy to set his out-of-office and close everything that could possibly give anyone access to him during the break.

Davey walked up to his desk, a glass of champagne in each hand, setting one down in front of Will. 'We made it! It's over!' he wailed mid-dance, keeping his glass impeccably still in the air. 'Come on Will! Get excited!'.

Will's head wobbled uncontrollably while Davey shook his shoulder violently. 'Yaaaay,' Will responded with little enthusiasm —although he did manage a small smile.

'Will, we're about to have two weeks of not this. You better get in the game, boy!'

'I'm in the game…I'm in the game,' Will replied.

'You're in *a* game…damn sure isn't the right game. We're going to go out and have some fun tonight. Celebrate a job well done… or left behind. Take your pick.'

Will laughed. 'I'll be okay. Working my way up to it. Just need a moment to catch my breath.'

Davey raised an eyebrow sceptically.

'It's fine, Davey. Once we vacate the premises and get some fresh air I'll wake up a bit. Just exhausted.'

'Will. You don't need to lie to me, buddy. I know what's got you all moody and that's fine. I'll give you a pass on that lie just because your brief buoyancy was soooooo lovely to see. It truly warmed my black heart. In the spirit of said buoyancy, tonight I'm gonna make sure we find you some buoyancy in other areas.'

Will kept a straight face as Davey danced suggestively in front of him for an amount of time that made colleagues stop and watch— unsure whether a lap dance or desk mounting was coming next.

Seeing no change in Will's demeanour—not even a twitch— Davey stopped and put his hands on his hips. 'Your dick, Will…

buoyancy in your dick…rising with the tide of a fair freakin' maiden! Jeez, do I need to spell it out for ya?!'

Will burst into laughter, the strain of keeping it inside becoming too much. 'Just wanted to see how far this would go, Davey. HAHAHA!'

Will downed his glass quickly—champagne not really being his drink of choice—before going for the coldest bottle of beer he could find.

'Not sure about the whole buoyancy thing but I am keen to spend a few hours out to occupy my brain for a while. I'll have plenty of time in the next couple of weeks for quiet contemplation,' Will said before emptying half the bottle in seconds.

'That's the spirit! We're going to take over this damn town!'

'Let's just start with slight enjoyment and go from there, Davey. That way anything else is a bonus!'

'Fine, Will. I'll take over this damn town,' Davey said with faux-annoyance.

'Standard practice isn't it?'

'Certainly is, my boy. Certainly is.'

Davey clinked his glass with Will's beer and continued to dance to the nineties pop tunes that played through the office at a needlessly respectful volume—Will lightly tapping his foot while bobbing his head.

Davey and Will left the office with the regular colleagues—Aisha, Alex and Mike—to celebrate two precious weeks of freedom before returning to work. They spent their time in the most casual way they could—sharing jokes and their plans for the break—while moving from bar to bar.

Will was pleased that the events of earlier in the week hadn't reared their head for a few hours until they reminisced on how cyclone Shenae almost cost them their jobs. That inevitably brought up *the encounter* which Will and Davey kept quiet while they were all so busy.

'Noooooooo way,' was Mike's reaction. 'How did nobody say anything? This is huge!' Mike lifted his hand for a high five which Will reluctantly engaged in with less than stellar enthusiasm.

'It definitely is,' Alex agreed with Aisha nodding along.

'It *was*,' Will poured cold water on the whole thing. 'It was a brief moment that flittered away like dust in the wind. The last vestiges of my heart given a brief reprieve before heading for the noose.'

'Jeez, Will. It's not that bad. Plenty of fish in the sea,' Mike said, slapping Will on the back—an attempt to regain some positivity.

'I'll never feel that way again, Mike. It was a moment trapped in time…' Will trailed off, brow furrowed, as he looked to the side briefly. 'A moment in time.'

'You said that already,' Davey pointed out as he giggled.

'No! The time! The freakin' time, Davey!'

All looked at Will like he was going insane.

'Bloody Shenae! She took all morning and into the afternoon. You were almost late for your meeting and I had lunch late.'

'And? We all had a late lunch, Will,' Aisha said, still very confused by what Will was trying to communicate.

'I went for a walk late. It wasn't my usual time. The rest of the week I went back to my usual lunch time and didn't see her. What if I happened to catch her at her usual time and was too early every other day? Idiot!'

'It's fine,' Davey patted Will's shoulder reassuringly. 'If that's the case, then first day back you can just take a later lunch.'

'That's if she's back there, Davey. Maybe she was a Christmas casual.'

'Is that even a thing at libraries?' Alex asked.

'I've ruined it all!' Will dropped his head to the table— immediately regretting the decision as the stickiness took hold. 'I could have had the girl of my dreams and lost it because of my stupid lunchtime routine.

'Sooooooo…bottle of red, Will?' Davey asked.

'Yes, please.'

Will lifted his head after a few moments of quiet contemplation of the mess he'd gotten himself into. At least he knew exactly what he needed to do first.

'I'm going to the bathroom to wash my face. I'm certain I caught something from the table.' The group laughed as Will stood and walked to the bathroom. *Let's just try and enjoy the night*, he told himself, as hard as that was going to be.

The rest of the night continued in the original casual vein. Will put in his best effort to enjoy himself as the group disbanded one by one. Mike went home, intending to go to the gym in the morning—which nobody believed was going to happen; Aisha was deep in conversation with a guy and was happy to keep that going; and Alex had another party to go to. Davey and Will finished the night as they usually did—Will happy to go home while Davey kicked on well into the night—and morning.

Christmas Eve was only a short few days removed from the final stressful day of work. Enough time to recover from the evening and mentally prepare for all the eating and napping that was in store.

Will realised he hadn't checked his mail for a while and after wading through the junk that was dumped into his mailbox he came to a strangely well-presented envelope—definitely not the standard Christmas card that would be expected around that time of year. Within the envelope Will was presented with a cream-coloured sleeved card, bordered with flowery gold patterns. *Definitely not a Christmas card*, he thought to himself.

Within the sleeve were two cards, the first making him shudder.

Together with their families

Audrey Francis

&

James Richardson

*Request the honour of your company
at the celebration of their union*

Will threw his head back and shut his eyes. 'Not a wedding,' he groaned to nobody. 'This is not what I needed on Christmas Eve. And it's only in two months. Ugh.'

After reading the finer details of the ceremony and reception invites, Will decided to call Davey to share his misery of a wedding seemingly being thrown in his face like an unwanted Christmas present.

'Sooooo guess what I got in the mail today?' Will asked— curious as to what Davey would come up with.

'A booze advent calendar where every bottle has a message with clues that lead to your future lover?' Davey answered.

'Good one. But no. A wedding invitation.'

'Nice. Odd timing, but nice.'

'No, not nice.' Will wasn't keen on wasting time on how terrible this was. 'I don't need a wedding right now. Well…in two months. But still, not nice. I don't even know why I got invited.'

'Oh please. You don't know what headspace you'll be in by the time it rolls around. Whose wedding is it?' Davey asked.

'Audrey,' came Will's emotionless response.

'O…K…it'll be fine, Will.'

'How will it be fine? There's no way I'll have a plus one so I'll be sitting in the back corner like a loser.'

'But you'll know plenty of people there.'

'Not many I overly want to be hanging around with, especially not at a wedding.'

'Maybe you can hook up with a bridesmaid,' Davey suggested.

'No offence to them but I'd rather be in the back corner, thanks. Maybe I'll just decline. Spare everyone.'

'Will. We both know you're not going to decline. You'll end up going, have a few drinks, loosen up and have a good time. Clearly you're wanted there enough to warrant an invite—despite whatever miserable demeanour you risk bringing to what will surely be the event of the season.'

'Definitely not my season, Davey. I'm already looking to avoid relegation and strengthen up in the off-season to go again later next year.'

'You know I have no idea what that means, Will. In any case, you might have your after-party plus one ready to go by then. That way you can get a little reward once you've passed the trials.'

Will laughed. 'I'm not counting on that being even remotely close to reality, but I guess I'll go and we'll see what happens… Why today, though? I had to open this up today. My timing's off everywhere.'

'Maybe you're getting all your bad luck in early for a smooth ride later on…or rough…whichever way suits. I, personally, would love to be invited to a wedding again. It's been so long. Not since… the incident.'

'Oh, you mean grinding on the married groomsmen at a very Christian wedding to see whose seemingly locked closet door would spring open in front of everyone? That incident? Now that was the event of the season. How many family members cut you off that day?' Will recounted the story while trying not to laugh.

'Seemingly plenty, Will. Anyway, it was overseas. Don't you know the postcode rules?'

'Not sure home-wrecking applies in that case, Davey.'

'Oh well. We live and we learn. I had a great time, just as you will at this wedding.'

'Okay. I guess I'll RSVP. Good talk, coach.'

'You're welcome, squire.'

Will returned to work after a somewhat relaxing—and mostly solitary—Christmas break. The relaxation was dependent on whether he could stop his brain from overthinking renewed possibilities following the lunch time revelation. He spent the first week back trying different times to take his lunch break in a desperate effort to sync times with an appearance from the woman he had connected with a few weeks prior.

Ideas had been thrown around by Davey—with increasing ridiculousness—however with absolutely nothing to go off, both had to admit defeat and pivot their attention elsewhere. For Davey that was returning to whatever event he was soon to be attending, whether that be networking for work or making an appearance to sustain his fabulous social life.

Will reluctantly re-activated his dating apps after taking Davey's advice to find a potential after-party plus one. In an effort to avoid the depression that always came with this venture for Will, he limited his time to a maximum of an hour a day of any interaction so he could continue to spend time with his passions.

The experience was as tedious as Will remembered. Swiping through profiles full of the usual quotes which infuriated him so much: "On here to get off here"; "Are there no more good men left out there?"; and Will's favourite line which added no value "Agree or disagree that pineapple doesn't belong on pizza".

A few matches came and went quickly—either because they had nothing in common or because they simply disappeared. Will was constantly reminding himself that every person is different so no lessons can be learned from person to person. *Once they're gone, they're gone. Just move on,* he reminded himself immediately after the match was ended.

With a month left until the wedding, Will organised a date after a period of enjoyable chatting with a woman named Lauren. She also worked in the marketing industry—as a copywriter—giving Will hope that they could connect on writing. She also supported the same football team as Will which was an added bonus.

Will was ready for casual drinks at a local bar after work during the week. His theory was always to keep things casual enough for a first date while giving a hard out with work the next day. That way a longer second date could be organised for a weekend if things went well, or awkwardness was avoided to end the date if they didn't.

'Okay, Will,' Davey had snuck up on Will as the work day neared its end. 'You all set? Need me to come along and sit nearby? Scope her out? Run interference if it goes downhill?'

Will laughed. 'No thanks, Davey. I've got this. It's just a chill first date to get to know each other. Appreciate the support though.'

'Still don't get why you don't just hook up with some hot mess on a Friday night. So much less effort and with all the drinking under your belt, all that awkwardness you subject them to will be skipped. Plus, being this close to the wedding it's a guarantee they'll still be looking for another round of "Will power" by the time it rolls around. Strategy that's guaranteed to work.'

'Hi, Davey. Not sure if you've met me before. I'm Will, aka the non-hookup guy. I'm looking for more than that.'

'In a month?' Davey eyed Will sceptically.

'Preferably beyond a month. As in an ongoing relationship.'

'Will, these are dating apps. They should be called hookup apps because it's all they're good for. Sure some lucky people may get a somewhat lasting sojourn out of it but the odds are sooooooo small that it will go that way.'

'So what exactly do you suggest I do?'

'Embrace the hookup, my boy. Embrace it and thrust it with your sabre.'

'So you have no suggestions for finding a lasting partner?'

'Not really. Maybe find a hobby that involves group activities and hope that the love of your life also happens to be there? That's a pretty big time commitment though. Might be easier to just plough your way through the nightlife going ladies and hope that one sticks around that you don't mind hanging out with,' Davey offered while shrugging.

'Thanks, Davey. Insightful analysis. I love the setting of the bar at its absolute lowest for some faux-happiness.'

'Always here for you, Will. Just consider it. Plough,' Davey whispered while slowly backing away. 'Plough,' he loudly whispered again.

Will finished work and made his way to the bar. Being quite early he got himself a nerve settling pint of beer, sat back and scanned his socials until the clock was almost ready to hit six. Managing to get himself into a state of semi-relaxation he was optimistic that the night would at least be enjoyable. Once past the awkward early stages, and worked out some quality talking points, he could settle, find his groove and get through without issue.

As the clock was ready to strike, Will got a bottle of water and glasses for the two of them and waited for Lauren to arrive. As ten minutes rolled past Will made a note that punctuality wasn't a strong point. No message to let him know she'd be late also wasn't ideal.

The next ten minutes came and went and still no Lauren and no message. As the stress began to rise he checked back on their conversation to make sure he had the right date and time—sceptical that he didn't as he added them to his calendar straight away, and it had only been two days since it had been organised.

Ten minutes again went past. Now half an hour late, Will was getting very frustrated. Benefit of the doubt was out the window at this point. Will picked up his phone again, entered the app and messaged Lauren. It was courteous enough. He simply asked if everything was okay and whether she was still planning on meeting up with him.

A few minutes passed and Will—anxious that he would come across as harsh—decided to message again with a light-hearted addendum. The words "Message failed to send" popped up on the screen as he pressed the send button. He tried again to no avail. *Maybe a bug in the app. Let's do the old close and reopen,* he thought to himself. Will re-entered the app only to be met with a blank "Matches" tab.

'What the actual fuck!' Will angrily said—the couple at the next table turning their heads and rolling their eyes at his angry outburst. 'She fucking ghosted me!'

Will stood and stormed out of the bar—annoyed at both the humiliation and the amount of time wasted. He made his way home and ordered some comfort food to be delivered. At the very least he could enjoy a delicious meal and watch a movie with his evening. While he waited for the delivery he called Davey to give him a quick update.

'Will? Did you butt dial?' Davey answered in quizzical fashion.

'She fucking ghosted. I was there for over an hour. A good half hour before she arrived.'

'And she definitely ghosted?'

'Unmatched as soon as I messaged to ask if she was still coming. I feel like such an idiot, Davey. I got pissed off and people started staring at me. I give up on this crap.'

'I'm so sorry, Will,' Davey's tone immediately more delicate. 'What an arsehole. And so am I. I pushed you to find someone for the wedding.'

'It's not your fault, Davey,' Will reassured him, knowing he'd take responsibility harder than anyone should in that situation. 'You just want me to be happy. I can't be angry at you for that. Too bad there's just so much trash in the world.'

'Can I do anything?' Davey asked.

'No. But thanks anyway. I just wanted to update you now before work tomorrow. I've ordered food and will chuck on a movie. I'm serious about being done with this, though. I'm getting too old for this crap. I'll go to the wedding on my own, get it over with and come home.'

'That's fair enough. Have as chill a night as you can and I'll see you tomorrow.'

'See ya.'

Chapter Nine

Jess

The Christmas break was relaxing for Jess and far more enjoyable than expected. She had updated Audrey on the previous two weeks' events which had filtered, in some form, to the entire family. This gave her a welcome reprieve from their insistence that she find herself a man for the entirety of the break.

As a result she spent her time off with books and brunches—along with an enjoyable few days in the wine region with Cait. It was exactly the break she needed to clear her head of the depression she had fallen into after the Darren fiasco, and her missed opportunity with the mystery walker.

As the return to work approached so did Jess' anxiety. Mondays were when Marie would make her weekly appearance at the library and Jess wasn't looking forward to a very unpleasant interaction.

'Are you okay?' Cait asked during their first lunch break upon returning to work.

'Really not looking forward to this afternoon,' Jess responded—her eyes fixed downward on her freshly brewed coffee. 'I don't know how I'm going to react to seeing her. I had the best break but what she did was disgusting. It's making me angry just thinking about it. Not just to me, but more to Darren.'

'Well if you're not feeling it just let me know and I'll take over.'

'Thanks Cait. Maybe keep an eye out to make sure I don't go into a rage either.'

Returning to work Jess anxiously moved around the room, fidgeting with whatever she could find as parents arrived with their children. As the clock slowly ticked toward the start of the session the room was uncharacteristically lacking in Marie's presence. Time slowed the closer they crept—Jess could even see the rest of the staff nervously watching the door anticipating the confrontation.

1pm arrived and Marie's failure to appear came with a relieved exhale from Jess along with a smile. Cait and the rest of the staff returned to their duties knowing there would be no need for an intervention. A wink from Cait suggested she may have had something to do with Marie's absence.

The relief morphed into a joyous mood—much to the enjoyment of the children and parents—as the buoyancy of Jess was on show in her reading, which kept all engaged. After all the anxiety of the morning, the afternoon could not have gone any better for Jess.

'See. Nothing to worry about,' Cait said as she crept up and wrapped her arms around Jess.

'You didn't at any point say there was nothing to worry about. In fact you pretty much guaranteed I'd be too unstable to handle it.'

'I also never said that.'

'The implication was there,' Jess laughed. 'So what exactly did you do to her while I wasn't here? Is she actually locked in a cell in the basement I don't know about?'

'Nooooo… It's officially a storage closet.'

Both laughed as they packed up following the final session of the day.

'Very strong words were had though,' Cait continued. 'Some officially from Jenny. Some not so official from me outside the building. To be honest I'm not surprised that bigot didn't show her face…and super happy about it. Now we can move on from that whole thing.'

'Yeah. I do wonder what Darren said to her though, if anything. I like to think he tore her a new one. I guess it depends on how the dynamic is with everyone around them. How are they even friends?' Jess asked in an utter state of confusion. 'She obviously genuinely hates who he is.'

'No idea, Jess. Hopefully he lost it at her after what happened and has cut her off. Maybe that contributed to her not showing up today. In any case—and I say this with the least amount of respect possible—fuck her.'

'Yeah. Fuck her. We'll all be better off without her around with that attitude. Imagine if I had told her we were together. She'd have an aneurysm.'

Marie didn't appear again as the following two months focussed almost entirely on the upcoming wedding. Jess took advantage of the attention being solely on Audrey and James.

Not being part of the bridal party, Jess was happy to help where needed, while avoiding any actual responsibilities. The only major task assigned to her by Audrey was a list of reminders she had to make sure James was on top of everything he needed to get done. It was a good chance for her to spend some one-on-one time with her brother that she didn't get too often in recent years.

James also appreciated someone with him that would give a direct, honest opinion without the fuss that came with having their parents in tow. The groomsmen weren't the most reliable either and also showed gratitude for having Jess to keep them punctual and on-task.

In reality Jess knew it was an easy gig. So much of the work had already been done so running a few errands, while getting the opportunity to hang out with James, was a dream lead-up to the wedding for her. Jess made sure the tasks were done as quickly as possible, which let them spend the rest of the time going out for meals or going to the pub. Sometimes with the groomsmen but mostly just the two of them.

'I'm so glad we've been able to spend this time just hanging out together,' James said to her the day before the wedding, as they had a final relaxing pint at the pub. 'We don't get the chance to just talk anymore. Weekends get railroaded by the rest of the family and I know they usually end up just pissing you off.'

'It's fine, James. I know you're busy with work and you and Audrey have each other.'

'Nah. I should make more of an effort to do things just with you. Talking about old times has been great and don't think I haven't noticed how easy you and Audrey have made it for me in the lead up to the wedding. I promise that I'll make more time for us after we get back.'

'I'd love that, James. Whether it's just us or with Audrey as well. I love you both so much and don't want us to drift apart. It feels like years since I've had time with my big brother.'

'That's because it has been years,' James confirmed. 'We used to go out all the time. Especially when you had a crush on my friends.' James laughed.

'I never!' Jess acted offended.

'You weren't as subtle as you thought you were back in the day. They knew not to mess with my little sister though.'

'So I've got you to blame for ruining my love-life?'

'Hey, if your entire dating pool was my friends then that's on you, not me.'

'Fair enough,' Jess responded. 'But unlike mum, dad and everyone else, you know I'm not just going to settle for anyone. You and Audrey actually respect that it's up to me whether I want to date anyone at all, let alone who I date.'

'Yeah. The oldies can get annoyingly pushy with that. Before I met Audrey I used to get it as well. They just did it to me behind the scenes. I keep telling them to leave you alone but they don't listen.'

'Nawwwww. Thanks big bro. Well by this time tomorrow you'll be a married man and I'll enjoy some gluttony at your expense, so I thank you in advance.'

'You're welcome little sis. I hope you have a great time but maybe it would be better if you were there with someone.'

'Shut up, James,' Jess chastised playfully as they both laughed. 'Cheers to your last day before tying the knot. I love you guys so much,' Jess said, lifting her glass, beginning to tear up.

'We love you too, Jess.' James clinked her glass. 'And I'm serious about hanging out more. If it's been a while I give you permission to have a go at me.'

'And I will take that permission and execute it at will,' she said with a broad grin.

Chapter Ten

Will

The wedding of Audrey and James had finally arrived. Actively avoiding any mention of relationships and dating—and focussing on spending his time doing activities he enjoyed—allowed Will to be in his best possible mindset. *As long as I make an appearance and congratulate the couple then it should all be fine,* he thought to himself on multiple occasions in the lead up to—and morning of—the wedding.

Given his recent physical changes Will decided a new suit was in order—also serving as a little treat for himself for deciding to attend. Turning up in an old, oversized suit also wasn't likely to help him in any way at that point or in the future. The new three-piece black suit, black tie and white shirt—along with a fresh haircut—left Will feeling quite good about himself.

It was a very short trip to the ceremony venue in the early afternoon of Saturday. The beautiful heritage-listed red brick building was surrounded by a small courtyard garden, hedges and a picket fence. Will took a moment to take in the architecture after sitting for a coffee at a nearby café until the last minute.

Entering the large decorative double doorway, the jarrah floorboards led down a short hallway into the main space. Plaster floral features and a chandelier adorned the extremely high ceilings providing ample, yet warm light into the room. A small amount of sunlight highlighted the end of the room via panelled bay windows which looked out onto another small courtyard of perfectly manicured trees, hedges and flowers.

Will weaved his way into the back corner of the room, which was almost at capacity by the time he'd made his way inside. He figured he stood far enough inside to not be noticed while being close enough to the door for a quick escape. His anxiety was building quickly with the small amount of space he had to move. The heat rose inside him as the summer heat still lingered. His exit route was clear enough, helping him keep his state at a manageable level. The advantage of arriving as late as possible was that he could also return to fresh air and space as quickly as possible.

Audrey's family occupied the first three of the ten rows of chairs on the side in which Will stood. He was keen to avoid a large portion of them until he at least had a stiff drink and a strategy to walk away. Opposing views had led to some altercations in the past and Will didn't overly want to be part of a heated scene— especially not at this point in the day.

James stood waiting at the end of the room with his groomsmen. An extremely large bouquet of flowers lay on an inbuilt bench in front of the window behind them. Will had never met James or anyone in his entourage. In fact he'd barely known of James' existence prior to receiving the wedding invite. Will and Audrey only had the briefest of catch up conversations in recent times and Will was quite surprised at receiving an invite.

The groomsmen donned suits in dark grey with a blush-pink tie. James wore a black suit with his tie tucked into a white vest. He was clean shaven with no need for a beard to accentuate a strong jawline. His thick dark hair styled into a side-swept look, purposefully opting for a scissor cut to keep some length on the sides. Will couldn't help but think that Audrey had done very well for herself—hoping that his look didn't come with an arrogant personality.

As the celebrant returned from outside, a string quartet in the front corner of the room began to play traditional wedding tunes, signalling the imminent arrival of the bride. All stood and Will realised he found himself amongst the tallest in attendance. The odd gap allowed Will a brief glimpse at different points down the aisle, although once everyone had returned to their seats he knew he'd have a relatively uninterrupted view of proceedings.

One by one the bridesmaids entered—each in a blush-pink A-line off-the-shoulder dress, spanning down to the floor. Each also held a small bouquet of flowers.

Finally Audrey entered the room to gasps by those in attendance —arm-in-arm with her dad. Will glimpsed a joyous smile on James' face through the crowd which was only matched by Audrey. Her dress matched the style of the bridesmaids—A-line off-the-shoulder. Although where their blush-pink dresses were simple in appearance, Audrey's dress was traditional white— intricately adorned with leaf appliqués—the tulle skirt trailing along the wooden floor behind her. The same pattern embellishments connected across her flutter sleeves.

Audrey's deep puce lipstick matched her dark auburn hair

which lightly curled down her back. The half-up style held in place by a smaller arrangement of the bouquet of flowers she was holding—notes of white and powder pink with a sprinkling of rich green leaves spotting the borders.

Audrey's dad handed her over to James at the end of the aisle and took his position next to his wife in the first row. As the celebrant began proceedings the string quartet faded to silence and everyone who was able took their seat.

'We are gathered here on this wonderful day,' the celebrant began, clearly a veteran of the profession, as she held no notes. The ceremony flowed through perfectly with only a few momentary pauses as each attempted to maintain their composure during their vows.

'And I now pronounce you husband and wife. You may now kiss the bride,' the celebrant concluded as Audrey and James sealed their marriage with a kiss in front of the cheering crowd.

After a brief break to complete the administrative side, the bridal party paired up and made their way back down the aisle and out of the building to a second chorus of cheers. Will joined the crowd as they made their way outside to congratulate the newly married couple.

Filing through, Will hugged Audrey. 'Congratulations, Audrey. I'm so happy for you.'

'Thanks, Will. I'm so happy you came.'

Will was moved on as the line continued forward. He shook James' hand and congratulated him on marrying Audrey. Having never met Will before, James simply shared his hand in return and thanked him.

Making his way through the crowd Will left the mass of people as quickly as he could manage and walked into a nearby pub for a pint of cold beer—happy for the space he was afforded between the lunchtime and late afternoon crowds. He'd made it through the first part of the day and could take a couple of hours to relax before the reception.

Jess

Despite not being part of the bridal party Jess spent the morning with Audrey, her bridesmaids and the mother of the bride as they prepared for the big day. They had spent the previous night in a hotel near the reception venue and enjoyed a relaxing evening with dinner and drinks—a final night of the pre-married life for Audrey before the wedding day stress began.

Her penchant for organisation ensured everything was in order and everyone's requests were met while their hair and makeup was done to perfection. Whenever anyone was getting tense she was able to rattle off humorous stories locked in her head from all the reading—and re-reading—she had done over the years. All were grateful for Jess' help as she left to get herself ready for the wedding and ensure that her parents had done the same.

Upon arriving at her parents she found her dad washing his car. 'Is it really the right time for that, Dad?' she asked him as she started unpacking her belongings to take inside.

'I've got plenty of time,' he replied as he threatened to spray her with the hose—a joke which only one of them found funny.

'Dad, if you make us late everyone will be lining up to kill you. You get that, right?'

'It's fine. You don't want to turn up in a dirty car, do you?'

'Dad, we're getting a freakin' taxi. We told you this repeatedly,' Jess replied as her blood began to boil. 'Get your arse inside and get ready.'

'Calm down, Jess. It won't take me long to get ready. How are the boys getting to the ceremony?'

'Not in your car, that's for sure. Don't worry about them. They've got their end completely organised. I made sure of that.' Jess had organised a limousine to take James and his groomsmen to the ceremony from James and Audrey's house—on her dad's credit card, of course.

Jess stood waiting for her dad to finish his final hose of the car to make sure he returned to the house as quickly as possible, making him carry her box of makeup and accessories while she carefully transported her dress inside. Seeing her dad enter the house with her, Jess' mum thanked her for dragging him back in. Jess knew her mum would have been stressing about being ready on time and wanted his help to at least keep her sane while she helped with the grandparents. On top of getting ready, they also needed to have their bags packed and by the door, to be picked up later, for their overnight stay at the same hotel where Jess was staying.

As a thank you for helping, Audrey had organised for Jess to get her hair done before leaving, meaning she only needed to do her makeup and get dressed while organising her parents. Always wanting to keep at least part of her fantasy book aesthetics, her light blonde hair was beautifully styled in a waterfall braid, falling down into soft curls. Small daffodils were weaved into the braid.

Jess opted for a peach lip gloss and soft blush to go with her light yellow, strapless maxi dress. The elegant panels of the soft chiffon dress crisscrossed over a sweetheart bodice before draping down from the waist. Her white strapped heels were each adorned with a daffodil on top to match those in her hair.

The extra large taxi arrived and with it Jess and her mum herded the family outside. After a quick photo—the driver kindly playing his part as photographer—they all packed in and were on the road.

Arriving at the venue Jess marvelled at how beautiful it was. Being an inner city venue she was worried that it would just be an old building hidden between the surrounding skyscrapers. As it happened the heritage building was on a corner lot allowing some of the land to be used for a courtyard garden. The garden also continued around the building providing an array of trees, hedges and flowers. Jess joined her mum on a quick tour of the outside before making their way inside. They had purposefully arrived quite early in order to get Jess' grandparents seated without having to push through a crowd of people.

James and the groomsmen arrived shortly after Jess and her family had claimed their seats in the first few rows on the right hand side of the room, before the first wave of guests began to arrive. Jess couldn't contain her excitement, running up to him and giving him as close a hug as she could manage without ruining his suit with makeup.

'You guys look sooooo good,' she squealed.

'I thought you moved on from my mates,' he joked. 'Besides, they're all married now. You don't want to be a home-wrecker do you? On my wedding day?'

'Very funny, James. I can compliment how well you've all managed to scrub up without there being anything behind it.'

'I know, Jess. You're looking great too. Maybe one of Audrey's friends will catch your eye this evening?'

'I highly doubt that. Anyway, I'm not on the lookout. I'm just here to enjoy your wedding. You ready to go?' Jess asked.

'Hundred percent. Memorised my vows, we've got the rings, reception speech is on my phone. We're good.'

'Yaaaaaay! I'm so excited. Now I'll stop hogging your attention. It's going to be perfect.'

'Thanks, sis. There's no way I would've been this prepared without you and Audrey.'

'It's my pleasure big bro,' Jess giggled and returned to her seat, allowing the rest of her family an opportunity to have their moment with James before the celebrant took his attention.

It wasn't long before the room was completely full. Jess wasn't sure where James was getting his intelligence from regarding Audrey's side of the room. Everyone was either far too young, far too old or both taken and not her type. *At least the small part of me which worried about that can get back in its hole,* she thought to herself, glad it was no longer a factor—or a distraction.

After another short wait the celebrant returned, signalling that proceedings were about to begin. Jess gave James two thumbs up and a huge smile which he promptly returned before focussing his gaze exclusively at the short hallway at the end of the room.

As the string quartet began to play Jess turned as well and the bridesmaids made their entrance—one by one. Jess was amazed at the number of people that had squeezed into the venue. It was standing room only at the back and filled with people.

The bridesmaids looked stunning. Jess had already seen the dresses and hair—and makeup was well underway by the time she had left—however she hadn't seen the final product until that moment. Taking a sneaky look back at James she saw him give a nod of approval as the first bridesmaid entered the room.

With the bridesmaids in place, the celebrant called for the room to stand in preparation for the bride's arrival. Unfortunately for Jess that made it even harder for her to see so she decided to watch James' reaction instead.

As gasps echoed through the room the biggest grin Jess had ever seen on her brother emerged, and she even noticed a slight watering of his eyes and blush of his cheeks. James' happiness warmed her heart as the moisture also built in her eyes.

Jess returned her attention to the aisle to get a glimpse of Audrey as she walked with her dad. Seeing the picture of perfection, Jess began to feel the desire to also experience that same walk down the aisle with her dad—a feeling she quickly pushed aside to fully take in Audrey and James' moment.

As Audrey was handed over to James, Jess had to stop herself from running over to hug them both—her excitement almost taking control. Her mum took hold of her arm, although Jess couldn't discern whether that was to settle Jess or to keep herself grounded. The instruction to once again take their seats was a welcome tonic to help them both remain in place.

So excited was Jess that she barely registered anything that was being said. Her gaze was transfixed on the couple—the smiles on their faces and love in their eyes—and the ceremony passed quicker than she had expected. As documents were signed Jess rested her head upon her mum's shoulder. She daydreamed about what her perfect wedding—should it ever happen—would look like.

Finally the time came for James and Audrey to follow the bridesmaids and groomsmen back down the aisle. By the time they had moved into the hallway Jess had almost lost her voice with all the cheering she was doing. Patiently she waited with her family as those in attendance slowly filtered out of the venue to give their congratulations to the married couple. Jess anxiously walked around the end of the room, closely inspecting the bouquet of flowers, to keep herself occupied while she waited to see her brother and sister-in-law.

Jess made sure to keep herself at the back of the queue to selfishly make sure she wouldn't get quickly ushered through. She couldn't contain herself, jumping on the spot in anticipation, while her parents gave their congratulations. Her mum—with tears streaming down her face—needed to be pulled off James by Jess' dad to finally allow Jess access. She jumped into both their arms, squealing and attempting to speak actual words, leaving Audrey and James laughing at her excitement.

'We're the ones that got married, Jess,' James joked as he moved his hands onto Jess' shoulders to hold her on the ground.

'I know but I'm so happy for both of you. I love you guys so much!'

'We love you too, Jess,' Audrey said, a beaming smile on her face. 'And we're happy you're so excited. Make sure you save some energy for the reception though.'

'I'll make sure to re-energise while you guys are all off getting photos.'

'Speaking of photos,' James interrupted. 'We probably should get the family ones in quickly since we need to head off soon.' James nodded to the photographer—an indication to herd everyone into their required groups to streamline the process of getting the family photos done.

Luckily for the elder attendees the process of taking photos was efficiently accomplished—the warm weather not making it the most comfortable of experiences.

'To the pub! Jess' dad called, to the cheers of many around him.

'Dad, No!' Jess scolded him. 'We need to go home and then get checked into the hotel.'

'Just one, Jess. We'll be quick,' her grandfather pleaded.

'It's James' wedding. If we're late to the reception he'll kill us-'

'Don't be so dramatic, Jess,' her dad interrupted.

'Fine. He won't kill you…but I will. Come on. We're going to get checked in and then maybe, if we have time, we can go to the pub. Not that the reception will be short of drinks,' Jess sighed.

Despite the protestations they agreed to follow Jess' lead as she promptly herded them home and packed the car.

'Imagine we turned up to the hotel in a dirty car,' Jess' dad joked, to glares from Jess and her mum.

'Nobody at the hotel cares about your car, Dad. You also only washed it last week. Just keep on task and we can get your old arse to the pub.'

The check-in process was surprisingly smooth, giving them ample time to relax with a cool drink before making their very short walk to the riverside reception venue.

Chapter Eleven

Jess

The family strolled over to the restaurant overlooking the river. Parkland surrounded the venue, which was slightly raised from the ground in order for the large balcony—spanning three sides of the building—to hang out over the water.

Fairy lights spread like cobwebs between the balcony and nearby trees, ready to create a warm ambiance in the surrounding area once the sun had set. A canopy of lights hung like a net over the entrance—guiding them up the steps to the glass doors.

Upon entering, Jess paused to take in the beautiful room. Wooden floors greeted them with old wine barrels stacked on either side. The bar began on the left—the length of the foyer—

and curved around along the front of the dining area. On the right, artwork and old photos of the area hung from the cream-coloured walls, interspersed with wooden beams from the floor to hold the wooden gabled roof.

A large seating chart surrounded by flowers stood upon a giant easel before opening up to the main dining area. Tables circled a dance floor in front of a raised stage where the bridal table sat. Vines draped down beneath flowers which sat atop the table before cascading down the stage.

To the left of the table stood a wooden lectern, a microphone attached to a stand beside it. To the right the three-tiered wedding cake was presented on a pedestal for all to marvel at.

The entire room was surrounded by windows down to the floor, which opened at various points to allow access to the balcony surrounding the building. Small tables and chairs scattered the balcony for those who wished to spend time out in the nighttime breeze that was sure to come—the section which spanned over the water given extra length for outside dining on any other day. Some of Audrey's family had already made their way out with drinks to take in the view while chatting.

As Jess continued scanning the room—taking multiple photos on her phone before too many people arrived—she came upon an area for photographs on the opposite side of the entrance to the bar. A table of assorted props sat next to a large standing box which faced a gold curtain backdrop. She knew, from the many recent weddings and milestone birthdays, that the box housed a screen, camera and a small slit where the printed photos could be retrieved.

Jess helped seat her grandparents on their table beside the bridal party stage before joining her dad to retrieve drinks for them all. Luckily, the seat assigned to her was between her dad and grandad facing the bridal table, meaning both a great view of proceedings and guaranteed jokes—in increasing levels of inappropriateness— would be in store for her entertainment for the entire night.

'Pretty swish setup they've got here,' her dad said as she arrived at the bar.

'That's putting it lightly, Dad. This place is beautiful.'

'Can't imagine it was cheap. A place like this with all the decorations. Take a look at the drinks available. Top quality stuff. I bet dinner will be amazing too.'

'Trust you to start running the numbers,' Jess laughed.

'Just saying, Jess. They went all out on this one.'

'Imagine if you were the father of the bride. If Mum had her way…' Jess raised an eyebrow to her dad, not needing to finish her accusatory statement of her mother.

'Lucky for me you kids are all independent these days. No need for me to ever dip my hand into my pocket,' he momentarily held a straight face before bursting into a laugh.

Jess feigned annoyance on her face. 'Hilarious, Dad.'

As they took a couple of beers and a few glasses of white wine to the table the trickle of arrivals increased—the scheduled starting time drawing close before the arrival of the bridal party a short time later. Aunties, uncles and family friends soon occupied the surrounding tables after filing through to once again say hello to the eldest generation of the family—some hanging around for some time chatting about the ceremony and the setup of the reception venue. Mostly they discussed Audrey's dress.

Soon the room became a sea of people mingling, getting drinks and finding their table. Some took the opportunity to get group photos in before their condition deteriorated. A few platters of canapés also made their way around the room—the timing perfect to appease Jess' rumbling stomach.

Will

Will's stay at the pub was relaxing. He slowly drank his beer while watching the cricket on the large screen. The air-conditioning kept the daytime heat at bay while he regrouped to take on the evening.

While some Will recognised from the ceremony made their way to the same pub, they weren't anyone that Will knew—which he was thankful for. The last thing he needed at that time was to chat and catch up with people he used to know before having to repeat the process again at the reception.

Begrudgingly, he left the pub and instructed to be dropped off nearby the reception venue. This allowed him the chance to stroll along the river in his own time and keep to himself as long as he could. Part of him felt guilty for taking the selfish route and feeling negative, however he knew himself well enough—and some of those that he would be spending time with—to know that his battery could only last so long. They weren't bad people—at least not all of them—just people he hadn't seen in a long time and he wasn't keen on recapping the last few years.

As Will reached the entrance the sun was setting enough for the mass of fairy lights surrounding the venue to begin taking effect. The ambience had a relaxing effect on Will as the noise of chatter inside was still being kept at bay. It was a coziness he wished he could spend the night in, as opposed to the claustrophobic mass of people he would imminently join.

Alas, Will was well aware that time was short and the arrival of Audrey and James was fast approaching. Taking a deep breath, he climbed the few steps and entered the beautiful restaurant where he would be spending the next few hours.

Initially he was taken aback by the venue, coupled with the decorations that had been meticulously added. This, however, was very much on brand for Audrey and should have come as no surprise to him.

Will took the opportunity to get himself a glass of red before scanning the seating chart for where he would be seated. He was happy to see that he was placed in a back corner, close to a door on the balcony for when he needed to escape for some air. Apart from a couple that he'd never met, the table was mostly filled with some mutual friends that he occasionally kept in touch with on social media, but hadn't seen in person for over a year.

They excitedly hugged Will and dragged him immediately to take photos with the most ridiculous props they could find. At least he knew they would be good fun for the evening as they slipped straight into banter like they'd never drifted apart. Although they enquired as to how he had been, they never expected a long story with every detail. All much preferred to share jokes and reminisce on old times.

Will managed to appease himself with some canapés just in time for the arrival of the married couple. For the first time Will managed to get a look at Audrey without being blocked or rushed past. She looked amazing, which Will had expected.

After the best man—who doubled as MC—ran through the order of events and other announcements, dinner was served. Will opted for the steak, which was cooked to perfection, with mushroom sauce, sculpted mash and roasted vegetables. Will was perfectly sated to get through the speeches and was quickly able to get a refill of wine at the bar behind him before they began.

As he walked the short distance back to the table he was able to briefly scan the room as everyone was seated. He swore he glimpsed familiar blonde hair at the opposite side of the room, on the table occupied by James' immediate family. *Don't be stupid,* he scolded himself. *There's no way that's her. You really need to let her go.*

'Will!' came a call from behind him.

Will turned around into the embrace of a middle-aged gentleman who had clearly gotten stuck into the beers early and gone back for a refill.

'Hey Travis. How's it going?' Audrey's youngest uncle was always a guaranteed wild time so Will was happy to at least be drawn into a brief catchup before he got too out of control. Despite his antics Will had enjoyed Travis' company on many occasions in his younger years.

'Things are great,' Travis replied. 'I got married last year and now we're here for a great time. You know I love a wedding. How have you been, Will? I haven't seen you in ages.'

Before Will could answer the MC announced that speeches were about to begin.

'Catch up later, Will?' Travis asked.

'Sure,' Will replied before Travis gave him another hug, picked up far too many drinks than could be safely handled, and scurried back to his table—allowing Will to once again take his seat.

Jess

As the plates were collected from their table, speeches were announced as being imminent. Jess had enjoyed grilled chicken with herb sauce and roasted vegetables before a fresh glass of champagne was placed in front of her by one of her aunties.

'Don't go too quickly there, Jess,' her grandfather advised, taking a sip of his own beer.

Jess raised an eyebrow in his direction. 'And how many have you had? Still able to count?'

'Still in perfect shape,' he answered before downing the last third of the glass in quick time.

'We'll see once it's time to hit the dance floor.'

'Just try to keep up, child. Wouldn't want to show you up by leaving you behind.'

Jess burst out laughing enjoying the back and forth banter, which was usually interrupted by someone fussing over him.

Beside her, Jess' dad was sorting through the notes he had taken from his jacket pocket as the best man approached the lectern to continue the evening's proceedings.

After completing his duties as MC—running through a number of messages left by those who couldn't attend—a mischievous smile crossed his face as he settled in for some lighthearted roasting of James, spanning the years they had known each other since school. He ended his speech with some beautiful words about Audrey and how happy she made James, leaving him—and most in attendance —teary-eyed and choking up.

Next came the maid of honour—quite a few champagnes deep and almost tripping over the microphone cord on her way up—to add some anecdotes about Audrey. She also finished in tears as she gushed over the bride and groom.

The closer the time came to Jess' dad's speech the more he anxiously shuffled his feet and fiddled with his hands. Jess laid a soft, reassuring hand on his forearm and gave him a smile which had the intended effect of calming him down. While he had no problem working a room, Jess' dad wasn't one to make speeches to more than a small group of people.

As James stood to give his speech both Jess and Audrey beamed. Despite his usual schmoozing of a crowd with jokes and a cheeky turn of phrase, James was all about the romantic words for his bride—after thanking his family, Audrey's family and everyone involved in the wedding. Walking back to the bridal table Audrey stood and embraced him with tears falling down her cheeks.

Despite having different speeches, both the father of the groom and father of the bride were all business—their words being near identical as they thanked everyone involved and welcomed their new addition to the family.

After the speeches were complete—along with a lot of toasts to the happy couple—Audrey and James cut the cake, before taking their first dance. Jess sat in her happiness for her brother and new sister, wondering what it would feel like to be that in love with someone and share such a euphoric experience. While she certainly didn't feel any regret for the way she lived her life, she did feel the desire to let someone into her life. The way they looked into each other's eyes as they danced with smiles on their faces spoke to her heart more than anything had done so before.

Jess' mum then danced with James as Audrey's dad did the same with her, followed by everyone else.

'Care for a dance, Jess?' her grandfather asked her, standing and extending his hand.

Jess looked to her grandmother.

'Go dance, Jess,' she responded. 'My knees struggle at the best of times and I've been enjoying this wine a little too much to wind back the clock on the dance floor.'

Jess took her grandfather's hand and followed him to the dance floor. His condition was only marginally better than her grandmother, although still good enough for an enjoyable slow two-step.

After a couple of songs Jess noticed a man dancing with Audrey and her heart skipped a beat. She hadn't seen him at all during the ceremony, nor had she seen him at the reception, although other than a bathroom break she hadn't left her table all night as food and drinks always seemed to find their way to her.

It looks like him, she thought to herself. *But it couldn't be. There's no way he'd be here.*

Her grandfather noticed her glances. 'You know that boy?' he asked.

'He looks very familiar, ' she replied. 'Although I'm not sure "boy" is accurate, granddad.' Jess continued to glance in his direction whenever she could. Manoeuvring them and craning her neck to get a better look through the mass of people on the dance floor. 'It couldn't be him, though. What are the chances he'd be at this wedding?'

'Looks like the love bug may have bitten you, Jess. I've never seen you so flustered over anyone.'

'I'm not flustered. Nor has any bug bitten me. It would just be a crazy coincidence is all.'

'All the people here you haven't seen in ages and you've got eyes for one man you may or may not have met? Whether you have or you haven't, it sure looks like you want to. Go dance with him. I think I've done all the dancing this old body can manage. You never know, Jess. He may be the man you've been waiting for.'

'You're the best, granddad.' She said as she escorted him back to his seat, eager to get back to the dance floor and uncover this mystery. An excitement and anticipation built she hadn't felt since her chance encounter months previous.

Will

Will sat through the speeches sipping on his wine and glancing at the large dessert buffet that was being set up nearby, strategically planning how he could manage a little bit of everything without having to unbuckle his belt a notch. An array of cakes, pastries, cookies and fruits spread across the long, covered table. On one side of the table a chocolate fountain had been switched on, surrounded by strawberries and marshmallows. On the other, a small portable freezer sat with tubs of gelato slotted into the circular holes at the top.

He barely noticed as everyone toasted the couple. While holding his glass of wine, his regular sipping just happened to fall in line with everyone else, making his lack of attention unnoticeable. It was only at the conclusion of the speeches where all stood up, did an elbow from beside him tear his attention long enough to also stand and join in. While he did feel guilty for not giving the speakers his full attention he was grateful for anything that would help keep his anxiety in check.

After the cutting of a large three-tiered cake beside the bridal table the dancing began—the dessert buffet still awaiting sliced cake before anyone was allowed to approach. Watching Audrey and James have their first dance made him reminisce on his wedding and losing himself to the moments of joy he'd experienced. He had made such an effort to learn a prepared dance and enjoyed a rare moment of dancing without thinking about people watching and judging him.

Unfortunately Will couldn't reminisce on the good times without feeling the guilt and pain of failure in his own marriage. It was all he could do to not bring that negative energy to the day and he'd made it further than expected without those emotions coming to the surface. The copious amount of love and joy in the room had become a struggle for him to embrace.

As Will stood to make his way out to the balcony for some air Audrey walked over to him—Will immediately hit with guilt that he'd distracted her with his black cloud.

'Come dance with me, Will,' she said to him, holding out a hand.

'You sure you want that?' Will asked. 'James will be wondering where you've got to.'

'James has a lot of family lining up to dance with him. He'll be fine for a while,' Audrey said with a giggle.

After a moment's hesitation Will took Audrey's hand and walked over to the dance floor. Putting an arm around her waist he smiled at her as they swayed to the music. Audrey was well aware that keeping it simple was the only way to go.

'I'm so glad you came,' Audrey said with a warm smile. 'I know this isn't easy for you but it means a lot to me to have you here. Mum told me she had to shut Uncle Trav up during the speeches, so he's happy about it too.'

Will laughed. 'I've never met a man so desperate for the power of a party to bring people together.' Will took a few moments to consider his next words. 'I'd be lying if I said I was completely happy to be here. Not that I don't want you to have the best day of your life, I really do. All I ever wanted was for you to be happy. I guess it just hurts to look back and know you looked at me like that at our wedding, and now it's with someone else. I failed you and there was nothing I could do to get that back.'

'You didn't fail me, Will. We both made mistakes. We put everyone else before us and grew apart. You're an amazing person and we all still love you. I wouldn't be where I am today without all the love and support you gave me. Unfortunately it's easier to see that when you look back.'

'It definitely is. I wouldn't be where I am without you either. We got through so many tough times. I guess we should've let some others take a share of the load. There's no point dwelling on that now though. We are where we are and we're at your wedding. By all accounts James is pretty awesome and all I can ask for is that he makes you happy. So as long as he's doing that then I'm good.'

Will was starting to feel the emotion rise inside him. Grieving for what was lost battled his joy at seeing Audrey so happy as it reached and constricted his throat.

Audrey smiled again. 'He does make me happy. He's a big goof but he's kind and gets me through when I'm struggling. So does his family. They're all amazing.'

Will followed her gaze over to her new family. Again he lingered on the woman in the yellow dress—his face a picture of concentration as Audrey looked back at him.

'See someone you know?' Audrey asked.

For some time he didn't answer, unable to take his eyes away as he tried to get a better look through the people on the dance floor. For a split second their eyes met and he knew for certain it was her.

'How is she here?' The thought voiced by Will.

'Jess? How do you know her?'

Will looked back at Audrey. 'I don't...I mean we kinda nearly met a few months ago. It's stupid.'

'Will, are you flustered? You're blushing.'

'I'm not. Don't worry about it. Today is about you anyway.'

'Don't do that, Will. Please don't let life pass you by because you don't think conditions are perfect. You have my blessing to go talk to her and if James has a problem with it I'll sort him out.'

'And James is her...?' Will asked.

'Brother,' she replied.

'Oh, great.'

Audrey laughed. 'It's fine. In fact you and Jess have a lot in common. You guys love your fantasy books.'

Will couldn't help but smile as embers of warmth began to spark in his heart—quickly extinguished as he remembered where he was. The quick change in Will's expression was not lost on Audrey.

'Will, I know you, probably better than anyone. I know the battle that's happening inside you right now. That sparkle in your eye when you saw her is rare, especially for someone you've never met. But I know you're going through millions of scenarios in your head, mitigating risk and pain, telling yourself you shouldn't be looking for love at your ex-wife's wedding. Your brain is rationalising keeping yourself in solitude and misery because of what you don't have anymore, instead of letting your heart be open to someone new. I'm telling you it's okay. It's better than okay. I want you to be happy just as much as you want me to be happy. You deserve that happiness without having what happened between us as an anchor.'

Will knew Audrey was right but the war raging inside him was too intense. His anxiety skyrocketed and he was beginning to panic. Tears began to well in the corners of his eyes as he strained to cut the rope that was holding him down. His glasses began to fog.

'Will… It's okay,' Audrey whispered as she hugged him.

Will's throat constricted and he couldn't speak. He hugged her back as James approached them.

'May I have my wife back for another dance?' James said with a beaming smile on his face.

It was all Will could do not to let the tears fall from his eyes as he let Audrey go, both physically and emotionally. Audrey was married to James now and while that hurt to acknowledge it was reality.

'James, this is Will. Will, James.'

James extended his hand as he put his other around Audrey.

Will looked down at James' hand and shook it, officially being introduced. 'Nice to meet you James. She's all yours,' he managed to squeeze out past all the emotion he was feeling.

Before turning away Audrey reached out and placed a hand on Will's arm. 'Please don't let your opportunities pass you by, Will. You deserve so much happiness.'

Will could only smile in response as Audrey and James turned and walked back to the middle of the dance floor. Audrey glanced back over her shoulder as Will turned and began walking toward the front door.

Will managed to open the door and make it outside before he burst into tears, the dam finally breaking and emotions spilling out. He jogged quickly into the park to get some distance so nobody could hear him as he broke down.

Chapter Twelve

Jess

Jess walked back onto the dance floor to find Audrey and James back in the middle, dancing together. Putting a hand on each of their shoulders she stared at Audrey with a panicked look on her face.

'You okay?' James asked.

'Shhhh!,' Jess waved in his face without looking at him. 'Who was that guy?'

'What guy, Jess?' Audrey asked. 'There's a lot of guys here.'

'The guy you were dancing with. The cute guy with the beard and glasses.'

'Oh my god, do you know him?'

'Yes… I mean no… It's complicated.'

Audrey and James both laughed, shocked at seeing Jess in such a state.

'Will had the exact same reaction when he saw you. All flustered. If he wasn't dancing with me I don't think he would've been able to look away.'

'I'm not flustered. Why does everyone keep saying that?'

'You're pretty flustered,' James chimed in.

'Shoosh you… His name is Will?' Jess smiled at that revelation, as small as it was.

'Yes,' Audrey confirmed. 'His name is Will and he's my ex-husband.'

Jess' face dropped. 'Your ex-husband? What's wrong with him? You never talk about him.'

'Well it would be kinda awkward if I kept talking about my ex-husband around James, wouldn't it?'

'I guess,' Jess agreed, her excitement halted.

'There's nothing wrong with him, Jess. We just grew apart for a lot of reasons. In fact you guys probably have a lot in common. You should go talk to him.'

Jess' smile began to return.

'Please tell me how you both know each other, but don't, and how it's complicated?' Audrey struggled to piece together their consistent, yet odd stories.

'He's the guy, Audrey. Just before Christmas when I worked at the other library for the afternoon. He walked past and we had an instant connection,' Jess beamed thinking back on that moment and that she now finally had her chance to make amends for her missed opportunity.

James suddenly burst out laughing although Audrey and Jess were both well aware he was trying in vain to hold it in during this entire exchange. 'You're in love with Audrey's ex-husband who you've never met. This is gold!'

Audrey slapped James on the shoulder. 'Don't start,' she said pointing at him, although struggling to hold in a giggle. 'It's adorable.'

'I'm not in love with him, James! I don't even know him. I just have a very strong curiosity at this time.'

James hugged Jess. 'It is adorable. Now you know how it feels.'

Audrey twisted her head and tried to spot where Will had gone. 'I'm not sure where he is. I can't see him. I think he might have gone outside for some air.'

'I'm going to go look for him,' Jess said as she broke out of James' hug.

Just as Jess started to move toward the door Audrey held her arm. 'If you really do like him, Jess, which you definitely do-' Audrey chuckled. '-then don't let him push you away because of me. It'll be his natural reaction to not go after his own happiness to avoid the possibility of awkwardness with me. I've given my blessing to both of you even though none of you needed it. Trust me, he feels the same way as you.'

Audrey gave Jess a warm, sisterly smile which Jess reciprocated as she started walking toward the balcony door.

'Jess!' Audrey called out. 'Out the front.'

Jess adjusted course and walked as fast as her heels could take her to the front door. She momentarily stopped wondering which way he could have gone. In front and to the left was a small carpark. To the right were the bulk of the fairy lights and a grassed area which opened out to the larger park space. *If he's the way I'd want him to be he'd definitely go right. It's so much more pretty and relaxing.* Having decided on a direction Jess descended the steps and headed onto the grass. Immediately she removed her heels to avoid any possible ankle turns and to increase her speed. *I'm not letting him get away this time,* she thought to herself.

Will & Jess

Will sat on a park bench, partially illuminated by a small amount of light from the venue and a nearby lamp. Being unable to shut off his mind in his panic, he decided on enough light for safety but not enough for any passers-by to see the state of him. The cool breeze from the river helped to calm him and catch his breath from the quick escape. His throat had relaxed and he was now able to breathe more easily, although tears still fell down his cheeks.

'I was so close to getting through under the radar,' Will said to himself. 'Guess I can't complain too much since I finally found her. I'll give it at least a week before I grovel to Audrey for her number.'

Will chuckled to himself at the odds that the woman he longed for was the sister of his ex-wife's new husband. His mind wandered through all the scenarios and permutations that could possibly happen in his endeavour of courting, knowing full well that none would be even close to what eventuated.

Why do I do this to myself? Stupid brain! Will took a deep breath. *This isn't helpful. Just chill.*

Will was well within distance to clearly hear the music being played at the reception. He closed his eyes and tried to give his attention to the music and let his thoughts float away. The tears slowed as he regained control.

'Hey Will,' came a soft voice from behind him.

Will quickly wiped his cheeks and turned his head to see her there standing before him, a warm smile gracing her beautiful face. He froze in the moment and his mind drew a blank for how he should proceed. *She knows my name,* was all he could think.

'Are you okay?'

'Ahhhh, yeah…yes…I'm great…thanks…and you?'

Idiot!

Jess giggled. 'I'm great too. May I take a seat?'

'Sure,' Will shifted to his left to make space.

'I'm Jess. James is my brother,' Jess said as she sat, placing her shoes beside her on the bench.

'Hi Jess, I'm Will…which you already know.'

Smooth, dickhead.

'Yes,' she confirmed. 'I made enquiries before I came outside. I'm not sure if you remember me but we almost met once before.'

'I most definitely remember. I'm surprised that you do.'

'Why is that?' Jess asked.

'Wouldn't think this random guy walking past would make an impression like that. I guess I did ruin the tranquility, though.'

Jess chuckled. 'Yeah, you did definitely do that. That's not why I remember you, though.'

'It isn't? And in my defence I was trying to avoid the dead leaves.'

'It was your reaction that I remember. You looked so sorry. You had no reason to care but you did anyway. I could see it in your eyes even from where I was sitting. That kindness is rare,' Jess smiled as she tucked some loose strands of hair behind her ear.

Will's heart skipped a beat as all the butterflies in his stomach suddenly fluttered in a torrent of activity. As they calmed he smiled at Jess. It was the feeling that both scared him—from the sudden loss of control—while simultaneously being what he'd longed to feel again with all his being. The feeling only Jess had been able to draw out from within him since Audrey.

That thought brought him back to reality—reminding him where he was.

'Maybe we should get back to the reception. I'm sure your family is wondering where you've gone and it is Audrey and James' day,' Will said as he turned his head to look forward through the trees, to the river.

Don't let him push you away because of me. The advice from Audrey entered Jess' mind immediately. *She would know him better than anyone else,* Jess thought. *And she was spot on.*

'Nah. They're all having fun. I think some fresh air is nice. It's a beautiful night. How about we take a stroll and you can tell me about yourself.' Jess stood and picked up her shoes before Will had a chance to respond. 'Come on,' Jess said over her shoulder as she walked toward the river.

A wide grin emerged on Will's face. *Okay, Will. No dicking about. No excuses. Forget everything that isn't right here, right now.*

Will quickly caught up with Jess and walked beside her. He put his hands in his pockets to prevent anxious fidgeting, relieved to have his phone in his jacket pocket.

'So Will-'

Ah crap. Will could only think of one place this was going to start —Audrey.

'-do you read?' Jess asked, smiling at him with a twinkle of expectation in her eye.

'Do I read?'

'Yeah. Like, books and stories.'

Will chuckled. 'Not what I was expecting you to ask.'

'Wouldn't want to be predictable, would I?' She giggled. 'What did you expect me to ask?'

'Honestly, I thought you'd ask about me and Audrey. You know who I am so I assume you know our past.'

'Is there anything I should know about you and Audrey? Given where we are it didn't seem like an issue.'

'True,' Will answered.

'I already know who Audrey is and she's not here walking along the river with me, is she? It's just you and me here and I want to know who you are, Will.'

Jess' tone was playful for what could have been a tense subject. This put Will's mind at ease despite scolding himself for immediately forgetting his own advice about staying in the moment.

As they reached the path along the river a cool breeze hit, causing Jess to shiver momentarily. Will promptly removed his jacket and placed it across Jess' shoulders with a smile, which she returned, touching his hand as she took hold of the lapel.

'Definitely just you and me,' Will said, the butterflies in his stomach helping to clear his mind of anything but Jess.

'Now,' Jess brought the discussion back on course. 'I believe I asked you a question about reading?'

'You ask as something to do with why you were at the library?' Will held off answering the question, both to playfully tease out answering and to hold himself back from a subject he was anxious to not be overbearing with.

'I was there in a professional capacity…and notice you've once again avoided answering the question.'

'Only for dramatic effect, I assure you,' Will responded.

'And?'

'And what?' Will couldn't hold back a laugh.

Jess lightly hit Will on the arm and giggled, the jacket almost slipping off, which Will caught and placed on her shoulders once again.

'Thank you,' Jess responded.

'You're very welcome, m'lady. And yes, I do read. In fact, not only do I read—a lot—I also write.'

Jess couldn't hold back an excited grin. *A lot in common indeed, Audrey,* she thought.

'And yourself?' Will asked, already knowing the answer. *Who asks about reading if they don't read.*

'Like my life would end if I stopped.'

'Looks like I'm not the only one with a penchant for the dramatic,' Will laughed. He'd relaxed far more quickly than he had expected and was already out of the "sounding like an idiot" zone that he was in when Jess had first appeared out of nowhere.

'It can't all be in the books, can it?'

'I suppose not,' Will agreed.

'And, good sir, what particular genres take your fancy? There are no right or wrong answers but be warned…some are more right than others,' Jess raised an eyebrow mischievously.

'I fear this road leads to dangerous territory. Does m'lady not wish to turn back?'

'Absolutely not,' Jess replied, the grin emerging once more.

'Well then, I say with the full embrace of the glory of nerddom that I love fantasy and science fiction,' Will eagerly awaited Jess' response.

Jess let the silent contemplation linger for more than what was a reasonable length of time, although her inability to hide the corners of her mouth from tilting upward confirmed to Will that she was intentionally making him squirm.

This girl is amazing, he thought as the anticipation of her response ate away at him.

'Hmph,' Jess turned her head away, feigning disgust and letting it hang in the air for a few moments before snapping her head back with a smile on her face. 'I love fantasy too,'

Will let out his breath with dramatic exaggeration. 'You nearly gave me a heart attack, Jess.'

'I guess I just would've had to bring you back,' Jess said with a flicker of a glance at Will's lips.

'And why would you have done that?' Will asked.

'Because, Will, we've yet to discuss a single book,' Jess laughed, as did Will. 'What about romance? Do you like a little spice with your magic?'

'Can't say I've stumbled down that path too often with reading, much less writing.'

'Who said anything about reading and writing?'

A sneaky sideways glance and smirk hit Will like a truck and he stopped in a cloud of awkwardness, having no idea how to respond.

This caused a burst of laughter from Jess. She was enjoying making him squirm, however more so she loved that she was comfortable enough to be this playful so quickly. It was far from the norm but she didn't even second guess it.

'It's okay, Will. I'm sure that mind of yours can craft some romantic plots,' Jess added.

'Oh really? And what makes you say that?'

'Because nobody calls me m'lady,' she giggled.

'Well I guess the limits of my spice and magic are here to be tested,' Will shocked himself with that remark. *Where the hell did that come from?*

Jess raised her eyebrows, herself slightly shocked. 'That sounds like a challenge, Will. Maybe we can make a romantic out of you yet.'

'Can we now?'

Jess only giggled in response.

The path along the river suddenly ended and cut inside. They stopped, both silently contemplating where they should go.

'Although we've come-' Will started.

'To the end of the road,' Jess finished as they both laughed again.

'Well, Jess. If we turn around this will be just the beginning of the path,' Will smiled at her warmly.

'See. I knew a romantic was in there.' Jess returned the smile.

Will and Jess walked back down the path toward the reception. As the two strolled they shared anecdotes from their past—light teasing not amiss in their conversation.

As they reached the grass clearing under the fairy lights both wished that the path had been longer.

Jess handed Will his jacket. 'It's been wonderful getting to know you, Will.'

'And you, Jess. It's been an unexpected evening.'

'Unexpected in a good way?'

'Extremely good,' Will replied.

Both stood smiling at each other in silence for a few moments until it bordered on awkward.

'I guess we should be getting back inside,' Jess said.

As she turned to walk back to the door one of Will's favourite slow, romantic songs started to play. His first thought—*strange time to play another slow one*—was very quickly discarded, replaced by *this timing is too perfect to miss*.

Will reached out and took hold of Jess' hand. 'May I have this dance?' he asked, a small smile masking the terror as scenarios ran through his head for how this one act could go terribly wrong—despite having no evidence all evening that it would possibly be the case.

Jess turned to face Will. 'I'd love to,' she answered with a beaming smile, throwing her shoes onto the grass a few metres away. Will did the same with his jacket.

Both being unsure exactly where the other stood they began slightly awkwardly, looking more like a couple of school students. By the time they were half way through the first verse they had slightly relaxed. Jess had moved her hand from Will's shoulder to his chest, Will's hand slowly moving to the small of her back from her waist where it had started.

As the chorus hit Will lifted his hand for Jess to spin. Giggling, she followed Will's cue with enthusiasm—rounding into Will's chest there she looked up into his eyes. Will began to hum along to the song as both were unable to prevent smiles permeating their faces.

The second verse continued as both relaxed further into each other. Jess nuzzled into Will's chest and closed her eyes, taking in every second, not wanting the song to end.

Will's hum turned into soft singing as the song neared the chorus and he could feel Jess' smile widen on his chest.

As the song came to a close, Will's heart soared as Jess lifted her head from his chest, tears slowly rolling down her cheeks—her smile never fading. Will let go of Jess' hands and gently wiped away the tears, returning her smile. As he finished lightly wiping her cheeks with his thumbs he left his hands where they were, slowly lifting her chin as he closed the gap between them and pressed his lips to hers with a care and love that flowed more than any could expect for two people who had just met.

Jess placed her hands on Will's chest once again, slowly gripping his waistcoat and pulling him ever closer, never wanting to let go.

As the kiss ended Will rested his forehead on Jess' as both smiled. A sudden cheer came from two people on the balcony. Jess spun quickly with more than a hint of embarrassment, Will's eyes also shooting across to where the cause of shock emanated.

Audrey and James stood watching, seemingly having taken a moment to get some air and a cool breeze while Will and Jess danced.

Jess and Will both laughed before Jess once again grabbed Will's waistcoat and pulled him in for another kiss, this with slightly more force and passion than Will had previously.

Audrey and James both cheered again then walked back inside, job complete.

Jess let go of Will and wiped gloss from his lips with a laugh. 'So, Will, what now?'

'Now we part-' Will answered, causing Jess' beaming smile to drop. '-for the evening. I'd love to see you again…and many more times after.'

Jess' smile lifted again. 'I'd love that too, good sir.'

They walked, slowly, to pick up their belongings from the grass, hand-in-hand, refusing to take their eyes off one another.

'I guess I should get your number,' Will said.

Jess bit her lip as Will fumbled through his jacket pockets for his phone.

'Got it!' he exclaimed, holding it in the air and causing Jess to laugh.

After giving Will her number he continued tapping on his screen for a few more moments, occasionally glancing up at Jess mischievously.

'What was that?' she asked.

'Just had to message someone special and let them know I might be off the market for the foreseeable future,' Will smiled at her.

'And who is this someone special?' Jess asked, crossing her arms.

'Just a beautiful woman I walked past one time and was stupid enough to keep on walking. She can really rock a yellow dress.'

'Hmmm…well maybe she was stupid for letting you walk away,' Jess replied before both she and Will laughed.

As they neared the door Jess turned to Will before ascending the steps.

'Tell Audrey and James thanks for me,' Will said.

'I'll make sure to do that.'

Will stepped forward and lightly stroked Jess' cheek again and gently kissed her.

'Until next we meet, my queen.'

'Until next time.'

Will turned and walked to the carpark, ordering a lift home on his phone, unable to wipe the smile from his face.

Jess stood and watched for a few moments until Will had walked into the darkness before returning to the reception. As she walked through the door Audrey scrambled toward her as best she could in her dress and shoes, James being pulled behind her although no less happy for Jess.

Jess pulled them both in and hugged them. 'Thank you both. Will said to tell you the same. I don't know what you said to him but that was a dream. I took your advice, Audrey. Thank you.'

'I'm just glad both of you are happy,' Audrey replied.

Jess' face dropped. 'My phone. I need to get my phone.'

'Odd time to obsess over your phone,' James said.

'Or is it?' Audrey asked rhetorically, knowing Will better than anyone.

They powered over to the table where Jess' bag lay and she quickly retrieved her phone. Taking a quick glance she held her phone to her chest, smiled and closed her eyes—Audrey mirroring the smile.

'What's going on?' James asked, confusion painted on his face.

'Well, James,' Audrey said. 'While Will can sometimes be on the awkward side he has a way with the written word.'

'What did he say, Jess? Or do I not want to know. Actually, I've overheard some of your book stories so maybe don't tell me.'

Jess hit James in the arm. 'Don't be so uncouth, James.'

'It's okay, Jess,' said Audrey. 'You don't have to say anything. It's personal.' Audrey smiled and pulled James back to the dance floor.

Jess opened her phone again and smiled at the message.

Your company this evening made my heart soar higher than any dragon would dare to fly, m'lady. If I were to leave this earthly plane now I would leave knowing I walked to the edge of perfection and felt her lips upon mine. I need nothing more to die happy.

'How the hell do I respond to that?' Jess said to herself laughing.

'Had a good evening?' Jess' grandfather asked, sitting at the table where she stood. She hadn't noticed him in her haste to check her phone.

Jess hugged him and whispered, 'Thanks, granddad. If you hadn't said anything it wouldn't have happened.'

'Anything for you, Jess. I could tell the second I saw you come back. Haven't seen you that happy for a very long time.'

'I haven't been this happy for a very long time. Added bonus is that everyone can leave me alone now,' Jess laughed as did her grandfather.

Nothing could take the smile from Jess' face for the rest of the night. Even as she ate a slice of wedding cake she was smiling. It remained fixed on her face as she returned with her family to the hotel and she closed her eyes to sleep.

Chapter Thirteen

Will arrived for his scheduled debrief with Davey the next day at a beachside bar for lunch and drinks. Will was still beaming from his evening with Jess.

Davey was already at a table outside overlooking the ocean, a look of shock on his face as Will sat down. 'And what the hell happened to you last night? You don't call, you don't write. I was worried sick!'

Will laughed.

'Will, I have never seen you smile like this. Ever. What the hell could have happened at your ex-wife's wedding to make you turn up in this state?'

'She was there, Davey.'

'Gonna have to be a bit more specific there, champ.'

'The woman on the grass near the library before Christmas,'

Davey pushed Will in the shoulder. 'Noooooooooo! Seriously?!' Davey's outburst drew stares from nearby tables. 'Oh don't pretend you've never had amazing news from a friend!' he called out, staring each of them down. 'I need to know everything… Wait… Drinks first and then not a single detail spared.'

Davey rushed off to the bar and returned with a cold beer in each hand. 'A bottle of wine is also on its way. Aaaaaaand begin.'

Will recounted every detail over the course of the next hour, occasionally answering a brief question of clarification from Davey.

'So you just went home?' Davey asked once Will had finished. 'Nothing else? You kissed her and left?'

'Yes, Davey. It couldn't have gone any better.'

'What. The. Fuck. Will? What happened to plough? Not even a light tilling of the soil?'

Will laughed. 'You have your way and I have mine.'

'Clearly,' Davey rolled his eyes and took a sip of wine, the bottle already empty.

'Bathroom break and then we strategise for next steps, okay?'

'Fine. Give me your phone while you're gone. I can find some cute dates for you to go on.'

'Why don't you use your own?' Will asked.

'Battery's dead. Had to occupy myself somehow while I waited for you.'

Will returned and Davey had a smirk on his face along with two more beers on the table and another bowl of chips.

'Now, Will. Before we continue I need to also partake in some news sharing. I may also be off the market for the foreseeable future.'

'No way! Please, go on my man.'

'Well, you know that night after work when we all went out and you left before the rest of us danced and I left with a fine, young gentleman?'

'Need to be a little more specific there, champ.'

'First, rude,' Davey feigned insult as Will laughed. 'It was just before Christmas. There were all those functions and then that arsehole got chucked out.'

'Oh yeah. I remember.'

'Well… Things have progressed very well since then and we're officially going steady, as the not so young people say.'

'That's awesome! Look at us having happy turns.'

'I know, right?!'

Will and Davey spent the next hour discussing hypotheticals and insane possibilities spanning the rest of their lives over some more food.

Davey's phone, which was sitting on the table, suddenly buzzed and he picked it up and looked at it before standing.

'What the hell, Davey? I thought your phone was dead.'

'Yeah. Kinda lied, soz. Anyway I need to get going because Darren is waiting for me.'

'You're just gonna leave?'

'Trust me, Will. Three's a crowd.'

Davey looked to his left, to the entrance of the bar and Will followed his gaze.

Will's jaw dropped as he saw Jess walk in. Her blonde hair in space buns—some loose strands framing her face. Sunglasses sat above her beautiful smile. She wore a red tank, three-quarter jeans and sandals.

'You sly bastard,' Will said, never taking his eyes from Jess.

'You're welcome. Have fun. Don't do anything I wouldn't do.'

Davey walked away from Will. As he passed Jess he said to her, 'He's all yours, girl. I can't wait to get to know you more.'

'You too, Davey. Thanks for the message.'

'Anytime, babe. I've never seen him like this.' Jess smiled at Davey as he left to meet up with Darren.

Will stood as Jess approached the table. She quickened her pace, taking off her glasses, and wrapped her arms around Will's neck. He lifted her into the air as they kissed and he spun her around, both oblivious to the stares from others around them.

Will lowered Jess and kissed her again. 'How are you going?' he asked.

Jess smiled, took a moment and kissed Will. She stared into his eyes, getting lost briefly before smiling again and answering with a single word. 'Perfect.'

Acknowledgements

Writing this story was so strange for me. I never thought I'd write anything outside of fantasy and sci-fi. Despite being part way into book 2 of The Tales of Matthew Parlour, a couple of brief moments of inspiration weaved this wholesome tale in my mind and once it took hold, refused to leave.

It's not lost on me the privileges I have in Australia in 2025 to be able to put this out into the world, privileges which are unfortunately not afforded to all. I respectfully acknowledge the Traditional Owners of the land on which I reside, the Whadjuk Nyoongar people of Western Australia, and pay my respects to Elders past and present. I also acknowledge the Traditional Owners of Country throughout Australia and acknowledge their continuing connection to land, waters and community.

I have to thank my writing buddies all over Australia who urged me to go through with creating this novella despite the genre being well outside my comfort zone. You've been so supportive through the entire process and your bubbly excitement has been infectious.

My beta readers, Amy, Jacob and Joyce gave their time to read my silly little story and provide invaluable feedback, both positive and critical, to helped shape what A Perfect Fantasy has become. You have no idea how much your words mean to me, especially when I was wondering what business I had writing this genre.

To my family and close friends here in Perth, thank you for regularly picking me up when I'm down. The road to get through writing this story, and all the way to publishing, was fraught with a lot of emotional speed bumps and you've always been there to listen and support and I love you for it.

My beautiful dog, Pikachu, who sadly passed during the beta and editing stage. She was there to lift my spirits through the toughest times in my life, helping me get through the healing journey that came with writing this story. She'll always live within my heart and those who had the pleasure of spending time with her.

I have to also acknowledge Michelle. You made me promise to never stop writing and although our paths have gone in different directions, you have always been supportive of me giving life to the stories in my head. Without your support from the second I decided to create a universe for Matthew to live in—which became A Dawn Left Behind—I wouldn't be here writing acknowledgements on A Perfect Fantasy. I'll always be grateful for you never questioning my desire to do this.

To the lady sitting on the grass that early December afternoon. I may never know who you are, or your name for that matter, but without those few seconds that our eyes met, Jess and this story would never have come to life on the page. It's funny how something so small can spark something much bigger.

Lastly, thank you to you, the reader, for allowing the story of Will and Jess to come into your life. While the journey of creating this book is rewarding in itself, having others connect with something that would have otherwise only briefly circled through my mind warms my heart. I'm forever grateful to you.

Mark Aeschlimann hails from Perth, Australia and is predominantly a young adult fantasy author, although inspiration in any genre cannot be ignored.

By day he builds websites for those who strive to make the world a better place as he has done since 2006. Themes of justice for the oppressed are ever-present in whatever he creates.

A long-time consumer of anything fantasy and sci-fi, Mark's adoration of fantastical world building has become a passion in his own writing along with characters whose complexity mirrors that of the real world.

For more information on Mark,
check out his socials and website:

@mark.aeschlimann
markaeschlimann.com